VINCE

ONE NIGHT WITH A MARINE

LISA CARLISLE

LISACARLISLEBOOKS.COM

JOIN MY VIP READERS LIST!

Don't miss any new releases, giveaways, specials, or freebies! Access EXCLUSIVE bonus content.

Join the VIP list at *lisacarlislebooks.com* and download *Antonio: A Second Chance Marine Romance for free today!*

Join my Facebook reader group!

Vince

Copyright 2020 Lisa Carlisle

Edited by Mellow Wood Editing

Cover by Talia's Book Covers

The right of Lisa Carlisle to be identified as author of this Work has been asserted by her in accordance with sections 77 and 78 of the Copyright, Designs and Patents Act 1988.

All rights reserved. No part of this publication may be reproduced, stored in retrieval system, copied in any form or by any means, electronic, mechanical, photocopying, recording or otherwise transmitted without written permission from the publisher. You must not circulate this book in any format.

This book is licensed for your personal enjoyment only. This ebook may not be resold or given away to other people. If you would like to share this book with another person, please do so through your retailer's "lend" function. If you're reading this book and did not purchase it, or it was not purchased for your use only, then please return it and purchase your own copy. Thank you for respecting the hard work of this author.

To obtain permission to excerpt portions of the text, please contact the author at lisacarlislebooks@gmail.com.

All characters in this book are fiction and figments of the author's imagination. Any resemblance to actual events or locales or persons, living or dead, is entirely coincidental.

Find out more about the author and upcoming books online at lisacarlislebooks.com, facebook.com/lisacarlisleauthor, or @lisacbooks.

Created with Vellum

VINCE

A Second Chance Marine Romance
   Lisa Carlisle

She has a rule. He has two problems. But can one night lead to forever?

Emma - I've sworn never to date another man in the military.

It's non-negotiable. Not only was I burned, but my mom, too.

Except the hot Marine I had a one-night stand with just popped back into my life as the EOD tech I'm working with.

Awkward.

Especially since Vince in real life is even more irresistible than the sexy stranger at the wedding.

Too bad it won't work.

It can't.

Unless I forego my one rule and let my heart be the guide.

But will it lead me to being burned again?

Vince - I'm only in town for a short time, but Emma wants nothing to do with the military.

Before my holiday break home in Newport, I'll be spending time with Emma--the hot caterer I had one amazing night with at my brother's wedding.

She's full of contradictions.

And I can't resist a puzzle.

Or a beautiful woman I have chemistry with.

I won't be here for long, so we can't enjoy ourselves for a little while?

But when someone breaks into her apartment, my interest grows into more than just being friends with benefits.

I need to ensure she's safe.

Can I protect Emma while shielding both of our hearts? Or will we end up casualties in the explosion?

Meet the DeMarchis family in this series by USA Today bestselling author Lisa Carlisle. Navy SEALs, Marines, and hometown heroes -- each encounters his most complicated mission yet when a woman from his past challenges his plans for his future.

CHAPTER ONE

VINCE

"'Til death do you part? That is one messed up mission." Vince gave his older brother, Angelo, a lopsided smile.

They stood before Narragansett Bay where Angelo had just married his fiancée, Catherine, in an outdoor ceremony. An occasional sea breeze rolled in with its heady fragrance, cooling the heat of the summer day. The sun had begun to set, painting fiery streaks across the sky.

"And he volunteered for it, no less," Vince's younger brother, Matty, added.

They all wore matching tuxedos with blue cummerbunds. Angelo and Matty had trimmed their hair and beards for the wedding, while Vince had his Marine-required clean-shaven face and close haircut.

"It's a marriage, not a mission." Angelo laughed. "When you find the right woman, you go for it." He nodded as if it was a solid declaration.

Vince and Matty exchanged a skeptical glance.

"That explains why it took you two over a decade to get hitched," Vince quipped.

Angelo grunted and smiled. "You know what I mean. We were kids back then. Our lives went in separate directions."

"Just giving you a hard time." Vince patted Angelo on the back. "Congrats, man. I'm happy for you."

His mother walked towards them with arms raised for a hug and smiling, although her eyes were glossy. Her dark hair was coiled without a strand out of place and she wore a blue dress with several silky layers. "Here comes Ma."

Matty covered his mouth and whispered, "Mother-of-the-Groom-Zilla."

Vince knew what was coming next. Since Angelo had announced he was getting married, their mother had been relentless. His engagement instigated many questions about when Vince and Matty would settle down.

"My eldest married!" She wrapped her arms around Angelo, and then attempted to pull Vince and Matty into the hug as well. They both leaned in to the awkward embrace with their mom as she tried to hug the three grown men.

"I never thought I'd see the day! What with you boys deployed here and there and it being almost impossible to get you all in Newport at the same time." She pulled back and moved her hard-stare along them like a drill sergeant. "Family is the most important thing."

Vince had been reminded of that many times, but he didn't blame his mother for repeating it. She was the one who was responsible for keeping their family together while their father had been out to sea, which had happened many times during his career in the Navy. It couldn't have been easy raising three raucous boys largely by herself.

"When am I going to see the two of you getting married?" Her eyes traveled from Vince to Matty.

Damn, that was quick.

"To each other?" Matty teased. "We're brothers! That's not really legal, Ma. Besides, Vince is too pretty for my taste."

She swatted Matty's arm. "You know what I mean. Everything's a joke with you. One day, you'll meet the right woman, and then you'll start to take life more seriously."

"Until then, I'll live the dream." He cocked his head and stared out to the sea with a carefree expression.

She pulled her gaze to Vince, waiting.

"Not going to happen while I'm in the Marines, Ma." He glanced out to the other attendees, focusing on his cousins, Jack and Antonio, from Boston, who were also Marines. He'd catch up with them more later, but for now, he had to escape the pressure to settle down. He deflected the attention to Angelo. "Now that Angelo's married, maybe you'll have grandbabies soon."

She clutched her hands. "I've been waiting to be a grandmother for so long!"

Angelo shot Vince an *I'm-gonna-kill-you* look.

While she refocused on Angelo, Vince stole the opportunity to escape as she could be more tenacious than a Devil Dog when it came to her sons.

Matty's voice trailed after Vince. "Aaand Vince disappears with his classic Irish goodbye."

Vince acknowledged them with a wave, but didn't turn back. He needed some space. He slipped inside the venue, an elegant stone seaside inn on the ocean. A woman with honey-brown hair pulled into a bun captured his attention. A strand fell across her cheek. She wore black slacks and a white blouse and carried a tray of cupcakes. He caught her gaze, and sucked in a breath.

Seconds passed and neither spoke. His heart hammered in his chest. He should say something, but he continued to stare into her wide brown eyes.

Where did all the oxygen go?

Her full pink lips parted as if she was about to speak, but then she tore her gaze away and shook her head as if confused. He blinked and inhaled, just as taken off-guard by his reaction. So what if she was hot? It wasn't as if he'd never seen a pretty woman before.

Still, he tracked where she walked. She headed toward the main room where the reception was being held. Guests were tearing it up on the dance floor to *Uptown Funk*. No way would he join in. He didn't get the appeal of flailing arms and legs like an idiot in front of an audience.

The ring bearer ran into the pretty brunette's path, followed by the flower girl.

"Watch out," Vince warned, rushing over.

It was too late. She tripped over the kids.

He managed to reach her before the cupcakes crashed onto the tiled floor.

Some of the cupcakes fell off the tray, frosting first, yet they'd salvaged the tray, for the most part.

"Are you okay?" He placed the tray on a nearby table.

She blinked a few times. "Yes. I didn't even see them coming."

His jaw tightened. Had he distracted her with his idiotic stare? "They came out of nowhere."

She glanced at the tray and straightened the toppled cupcakes. "Crap."

"You're down a few troops, but I think they can be salvaged." He picked up a couple of cupcakes and placed them upright.

She gazed at him as if perplexed and then shook her head. "Thanks." She brushed the hair out of her face but managed to smear white frosting on her cheek.

A chuckle burst out of him without warning as the ridiculousness of the situation caught up. Here he was in a monkey suit at his brother's wedding with a beautiful woman and fallen cupcakes.

"What's so funny?" Her brows furrowed.

He reached out and wiped some frosting off her cheek, displaying it on his finger tip. "Just a little frosting."

"Oh!" Her cheeks turned pink. "I'm a hot mess."

He chuckled. "Hot, yes. But not a mess."

"Thanks, I guess." She picked up one of the cupcakes off the floor. With a wry grin, she asked, "Have a sweet tooth?" She raised the cupcake toward his cheek as if ready to smear him.

He stopped laughing and waved his hands in surrender. "No, I can't mess up this tux. It's a rental I have to return tomorrow."

"Fine." She conceded with a tilt of her head and a sassy grin. "But, only because you helped me avoid a catastrophe." She tossed the cupcake in the garbage and used a rag to wipe the remaining frosting off the floor.

"At a wedding no less, that's colossal confectionery carnage."

"That's quite the alliteration over a cupcake collision." Her eyes twinkled and her lips curled into a demi-smile.

Wordplay? Hell yes. Nothing hotter than verbal foreplay. How could he keep them talking?

Ah, he'd be a gentleman and offer to help. He lifted the tray from the table. "Where can I bring these?"

"You don't have to do that. It's what I'm here for."

"Not a problem. I'm the best man. I can at least do something more useful than standing around in this penguin suit."

"Okay then. This way." She led him to a table where a white three-tier wedding cake stood. "We'll put the cupcakes on either side of the cake."

He stared at the selection. "Cake and cupcakes? I've already been hit with a sugar rush."

"*Everybody* loves cupcakes. Trust me, they'll likely be all gone while the cake will remain barely touched."

He shrugged. "You're the expert."

While she went to the kitchen, he debated his next move. Would it be wrong to hit on the caterer at Angelo's wedding?

When she returned, he said, "I'm Vince. I apologize for my family and friends in advance. An Italian and Armenian family and a Navy crew. Who will be the loudest and most boisterous is a tough call."

She grinned. "I'm Emma. This isn't my first wedding. I think I've seen it all."

Might as well hone in. "To make up for a loud night and messy cleanup ahead, how about I take you out tomorrow, Emma?"

Maybe not the slickest segue, but it was out there.

She eyed him, studying his face. In the few seconds that followed, his pulse quickened.

"Sorry, but I don't date military."

Damn. Shot down. Still, he wasn't ready to retreat yet. "How do you know I'm military?"

"Your haircut announces it like a billboard in Times Square. And like you said, a Navy crew is here tonight."

True. Although he'd let it grow before the wedding, the signature high-and-tight style still gave him away. "Not Navy." He took smug satisfaction in announcing that separation, just as he and his brothers had ribbed each other a thousand times. "Marine."

"Even worse!" She snorted. "Do I need to get an extra place setting for your ego?" she added with a flirtatious smile.

"No, I left it on base while I'm on leave." He stepped closer to her. "Which means I'm alone and could use some company."

She arched her brow. "Your family will be happy to accommodate that request, I'm sure." She turned with her tray of cupcakes and walked away from him.

Screw it, he manned up and gave it another shot. "I'd much rather talk to you, Emma. What time are you done here?"

She turned over her shoulder and gazed at him with an amused expression. "Around midnight."

"Meet me for a drink." He made a point of making a statement, not asking a question.

She appraised him with a lingering glance. "A drink?"

"Right. Not a date, just a drink. You can't leave me hanging on the night of my brother's wedding, can you?" he cocked his head and shrugged with mock innocence.

She bit her lip. "I'll think about it."

It wasn't a no. With the appreciative glimmer in her eyes, he'd put his money on yes.

"Until the witching hour." He gave her a half bow and turned away. Confidence was critical for any victory.

More alliteration. Amusement tugged at his lips. If luck was on his side, he'd have an unforgettable night with Emma, the cupcake caterer.

EMMA

Emma's eyes flickered open. The bands of sunlight drifting onto the burgundy arm chair and dark polished desk confirmed her little indiscretion last night. She was in a hotel room. Oh no. She winced. What had she been thinking?

Starting a new life in Newport would not go well by:

1) Breaking her rule about avoiding military men.

2) Sleeping with one of her friend's clients.

She glanced over at the Marine sharing the bed. Vince was hot. Last night had been pretty amazing—especially following her dry spell. Her divorce had turned her off dating and drama.

With long slow breaths, he appeared to be in a deep sleep. She pegged him to be in his late twenties, but without any tension on his face as he slept, he appeared even younger, like a college student.

He lay on his stomach and had arms rested on either side of his head. She paused to get a good look at him unobserved. Dark hair cut short, chiseled face, muscular body, and sensual lips. And that scent—all masculine and oh-so delicious. How could she have resisted? Last night in a tux, he'd been irresistible and now with nothing but the sheet covering the lower part of his body, all the smooth muscles in his back and shoulders stood out. An urge to run her hands over them again made her fingers itch. She yanked them to her side.

He wasn't a college student, he was a Marine. Even worse! The eagle, globe, and anchor and barbed wire tattooed on his biceps silently blared that announcement. She was all set with men in the military for good reason—especially after her ex's latest announcement.

Why was she lingering? She had to get out of there.

Careful not to wake Vince, she slid out from under the sheets. She found her clothes discarded on the floor and carried them into the bathroom. No, she couldn't risk waking him by making any noise. She quickly dressed and slowly turned the doorknob. Before she exited, she took one last look at him. A flicker of regret swirled. Too bad he was only in town for a wedding and not a regular guy living here in Newport.

His back rose and fell with deep breathing, so she didn't appear to have roused him. She slipped out the door, and then closed it behind her before rushing through the corridor and down the stairs of the opulent hotel, a near gallop of shame.

What was she thinking? The ink on the divorce papers was probably still wet, although her marriage to Peter had fallen apart last fall. She was a wreck from it, lugging too much emotional baggage to even consider taking on a hot lover like Vince.

After she freshened up in a restroom near the lobby, she booked an Uber. While she waited the four, glacier-slow minutes for her driver to arrive, she paced the well-tended grounds and fidgeted with her necklace, a silver shamrock she'd picked up in Ireland for good luck. To maintain distance from the wedding guests and stay far from view, she steered close to a flower bed along the side of the hotel. They wore fine Sunday morning clothes the morning after a wedding, while she wore clothes from the night before—black slacks and a white blouse—a telltale sign that one of the catering crew didn't make it home last night.

Ugh. Agreeing to help at this wedding had been a bad idea. It was too close to her divorce. She'd once repeated vows like that to Peter, and he to her. She grunted. That didn't turn out as promised—their marriage had crumbled on its shaky foundation of incompatibility and infidelity.

That near cupcake catastrophe with a dashing stranger last night had made her feel things she hadn't in so long. She'd been swept into the escape of one fiery night with the best man, even if he was against her rules. The way he talked to her and looked at her made her feel desired, wanted, like one of these well-tended flowers in this aromatic flowerbed. Not like how she'd been neglected by Peter's wandering gaze—she might as well have been an eyesore to him.

She glanced up at the stone seaside hotel again, trying to track which window was Vince's. A pang of guilt hit her, as she'd left without a note or a goodbye.

Perhaps that was wrong.

No, he was just another guy who only wanted one thing—and from as many women who would give it to him.

When her ride arrived, she dashed down the pebbled walkway and into the backseat. After she climbed in, and they drove away, she glanced back. Vince was only in town for his brother's wedding.

She'd never see him again.

SIX MONTHS LATER...

Emma grabbed a cup of coffee and sat at her desk, sifting through emails. Although she'd finished her four years in the

Navy earlier that year, this job as a civilian at the Naval War College was a good fit. Besides, it allowed her to stay in Newport.

Much of her duties focused on event planning and working in the library. A conference with numerous guest speakers was on the schedule for this week, her first big event.

"Let's get the speakers settled in," Emma's supervisor, Michael, said when he stopped by her desk.

"All right," she agreed and joined him as they walked down the hall.

"Then head down to check people in at reception."

When they entered the reception area, there were more than just a few who'd arrived early. Several small groups of people in military uniform and civilian gear stood chatting.

"I'm going to talk to the Captain," he nodded. "The EOD tech is over there." He pointed to a small group chatting.

She headed over and glanced at name tags of those in uniform to try to find the Marine she'd communicated with via email. No luck. She walked around those who had arrived. "Staff Sergeant DeMarchis?"

"Yes?" a deep voice called.

A man moved through the crowd from a dozen or so feet away with the short-cropped hair of a Marine. When he stepped into her line of vision, a gasp leaped from her throat. She squelched it and attempted to cover the sound as if taking a deep breath.

No. Noooo....

Dark eyes pinned her with a gaze as surprised as her own before it was quickly replaced by a neutral expression, revealing nothing. She'd never forget those intense eyes—they'd captured her from across the room when they'd first met, as if they were in some Frank Sinatra song.

It was him. Vince. The Marine she'd slept with after the wedding six months ago. Instead of a tux, he wore cammies. She had a sudden wish for camouflage herself so she could slip away. When she stole another glance at him, she had to admit he filled out his uniform well.

He stood about half a foot taller than her, so close to six feet, and his hair was now shorter than it had been at the wedding, trimmed to the Marine regulated cut. She pictured the fit body beneath the uniform that she'd touched in the hotel last summer. Heat rose in her cheeks as she struggled to force the image of his naked body away.

"I'm Staff Sergeant DeMarchis," he declared. "And you are?" he posed with a quirk of his brows. The hint of amusement in his voice rang clear.

As far as she was concerned, there wasn't anything amusing about this situation. She forced herself to state her name without stammering. "Emma. Emma Bradford."

He offered his hand. "Nice to meet you, Ms. Bradford."

She accepted his hand, ignoring the tingles that sent a ripple of heat up her arm. A flash of how he'd touched her with those warm, skillful hands returned.

Don't think it. Don't remember it!

"Emma. Just call me Emma."

"Emma," he repeated in a smooth velvety voice.

Argh, why did he make it sound so sensual?

"What a pleasure to meet you." His voice was laced with enjoyment.

She rose to her tiptoes and leaned close to his ear, unfortunately catching his clean, male scent that was all too alluring. She whispered, "This isn't funny."

"Funny?" Vince cocked his head. "I'd say fortuitous." He raised his brows with the hint of a challenge in his eyes. Those deep, dark, all-too-dangerous eyes.

A reminder of their verbal flirting with alliteration returned. "Definitely not. Whatever you're thinking, nope."

His eyes widened with mock innocence. "What I'm thinking?" His lips quirked into a semi-grin. "What is it *you* think *I'm* thinking about, Emma?"

All sorts of sordid images swam in her mind. She crossed her arms and grimaced. "I don't even want to think about it."

"Since it looks like we're working together while I'm in town, we'll have plenty of time to converse." He appraised her with a speculative gaze that bordered on smoldering.

Damn, this was going to be awkward. She took a deep breath and forced a smile. "Looking forward to it," she lied.

CHAPTER TWO

VINCE

*V*ince dressed in sweats to get ready for a run. The December breeze along the ocean would be brisk. A knock was followed by a familiar voice, "Hey, DeMarchis."

After he opened the door of his room at the Navy base, Grady greeted him with the standard guy nod. Grady was one the Navy guys Vince trained with the past few weeks at the Naval War College in Newport.

"Hey, Demo, I heard you're a tech whiz," Grady said.

Vince's nickname in the Corps traveled fast. Marines loved to twist a name. DeMarchis quickly became Demo, short for demolition. It could have been worse. His brother Matty was pegged as Demon, and Vince knew a poor schmuck stuck with shitbird.

"What's up, Grady?"

"My laptop showed me the blue screen of death and I can't get it to come on."

"I'll take a look at it."

"Cool." Grady raised his chin. "We're gonna grab a beer. You in?"

"Maybe later. I'm gonna head out for light run."

"We had PT this morning, hard ass." A grin spread across Grady's face.

"It's what separates the men from the boys," Vince countered. "Where you gonna be?"

"That may change as the night goes on. We'll start off down at Bowen's Wharf. Text me."

Once Grady left, Vince put on his sneakers. It had been a long day of classes and he could use some time alone to decompress and stretch out his muscles. He wanted to soak in the salty ocean air while he was in Newport, despite the December chill. At least leave was coming up, and he'd be able to spend Christmas here with his family.

He headed outdoors and into a jog. The sun had already started to set, courtesy of the short winter days.

The military was a small world and Newport was even smaller, but to be paired up with the woman he'd hooked up with at his brother's wedding seemed like an odd coincidence. He released a low, skeptical laugh. Brilliant.

It figured. The training program had been intense. All he had left to do were a couple of presentations—one at the War College tomorrow and another at a high school next week. Those were supposed to be the easy parts before leave. Now that he'd be working with Emma, it made things more interesting. She'd distracted him since they ran into each other.

As he quickened the pace, his heartbeat quickened and breathing turned more rapid. A fine sheen of sweat built on his skin, despite the strong ocean breeze. He glanced out at the dark water with the lights twinkling on it and shook his head. How funny that they'd exchanged a few emails while organizing these speaking engagements, not realizing they knew each other. Intimately.

He didn't know why she snuck out that next morning. She hadn't scrawled a quick note—not even a *Thanks for the Wham-Bam-Thank-You-Man.*

Why not? He'd thought they had a damn good night together.

As he passed by the next housing complex, he groaned. He should have been happy not to deal with any awkwardness the morning after and avoid any uncomfortable chats about staying in touch. For some inexplicable reason, he wasn't.

Instead, he'd attempted to disassemble every minute of the night to try to pinpoint if he'd done something to trigger her to bolt. He couldn't help it. That's how he was wired. He was fascinated by taking things apart to see what made them tick, and it was what made him good in his field. An explosive ordnance disposal tech had to be patient and steady and be able to dismantle something that could blow up in his face by making the wrong move. It was the perfect fit for him, even if it was dangerous and stressful. So many techs burned out from it, and he had many doubtful moments about how long he could handle himself. That was normal, explainable by human nature.

What wasn't as simple to understand was why a woman who seemed to have a pleasurable night with him slipped away as silent as a shadow.

He'd see her again tomorrow. Would he finally get an answer to that question?

EMMA

Emma bit her lip. This couldn't be happening. She trekked through downtown Newport after work on Friday. The bright lights of her friend Karine's catering business came into view, where Emma had worked last summer, and still helped out when Karine needed extra hands.

After Emma opened the door and announced her arrival,

Karine appeared from deep in her kitchen, which was full of stainless steel tables of different sizes. The scent of cinnamon baked goods perfumed the shop, and a Nina Simone album was playing. Karine often listened to slow croons or classical music while she worked, saying she needed tranquility in her workspace since her home was no longer as calm as it had been. Introducing a baby girl into her world would do that.

Karine stepped behind the display case at the front of the shop, which featured some of her top dessert sellers, like the cupcakes she was known for and even had catering requests from out of state. Her dark hair was pulled back into a messy bun, and she wiped her hands on her white apron. She pinned Emma with a probing gaze. "What's the issue you texted about?"

Emma grimaced and shuffled on the tile floor. "Have you ever done something you thought would stay far in your past? But then it sneaks up on you with repercussions you never imagined?"

Karine's eyes narrowed. "What happened?"

Emma tapped her mouth. "I'm a little nervous about telling you."

"Emma?" Karine's voice took on a what's-going-on tone.

"Last summer, when I was helping you with all those weddings, well…" She rubbed the seam of her jeans and her gaze drifted to the printed catering menu, avoiding meeting Karine's eyes. "So, I met this guy. And, uh, one thing led to another…"

"And?"

Emma sighed. "We hooked up." She lifted her eyes to meet Karine's judgment.

"Oh." Her tone was matter-of-fact.

"You're not mad?"

"Should I be? Was he the groom?"

"No, the best man."

Karine shrugged. "So what?"

VINCE

"I thought you might give me a hard time for sleeping with the client's family or something like that."

"Honey, I've catered enough weddings to see more hookups than fastenings on a wedding dress." Karine walked over to a drying rack where she removed stainless steel pans and placed them in a stack beneath one of the tables. "If you'd slept with the groom, yes, *that* would be an issue. You know, ruining the wedding of a paying client. I'm assuming he was single?"

Emma's shrug ended with a squeamish roll of her shoulders. He better not be married. "He wasn't there with anyone."

"Well then, good for you." Karine pulled out a chocolate frosted cupcake from inside a display case. "It's about time you had some sugar in your bowl." She laughed at the reference to the song playing as she handed Emma the cupcake. "I can't believe you didn't tell me, especially since you haven't mentioned any guy since Peter."

The back of Emma's neck tightened. "I was a mess at the time." She accepted the cupcake.

"Who wouldn't be after finding out their husband knocked up another woman? Besides the divorce, you had also just gotten out of the Navy. Huge, stressful life changes."

"It was definitely a perfect storm of stressors." Emma sighed. "Thanks for not being judgy. I was pretty screwed up at the time."

Emma had been trying to start a new life in Newport after the previous version she'd planned had crashed with epic collateral damage.

"I think you were allowed to be a bit off balance."

Emma stared at the frosted cupcake in her hand without any appetite to take a bite. That was how her little indiscretion had started. "Here's the thing. My one-night fling has turned out to have some lag time."

"Oh? How?" Karine's dark eyes widened with delight.

"A guy I've been emailing about a lecture tomorrow and a visit the high school next week—well, take a guess."

"No!" A snort-laugh escaped Karine, and she covered her mouth. "The same guy?"

"Yes." Emma's reply had far less amusement. "It looks like my attempt to keep things simple and uncomplicated have shifted with Twister-like contortions."

Karine made a sound of acknowledgment. "How did he react when he saw you?"

The ring of a bell and the door opening caught Emma's attention. A woman with blonde hair in a ponytail, who appeared to be in her late thirties, entered the shop. Karine moved to greet her and Emma stepped out of the way. After Karine filled a box with half-a-dozen cupcakes and took care of the transaction, the woman thanked her and left the shop, bell ringing behind her.

Karine planted her hands on her hips. "Where were we?"

"You asked how he reacted."

"Oh, yes."

Emma put the cupcake down on the counter. "He seemed as surprised as I was at first, but then amused."

"Hmm. Amused?" Karine tilted her head. "I wonder why."

"Who knows? I freaked out in the morning and booked it out of there without saying goodbye."

"Maybe he wants to hook up again." Karine's eyes glimmered with a naughty glint. "Will you go for it?"

"No!"

"Why not?" Karine's tone was incredulous.

"It would be super unprofessional at my new job. Guys in the military spread rumors quicker than middle school girls. I don't need to give them any ammunition."

Karine gestured with a relaxed wave. "You're out of the Navy now. Who cares what they think?"

Emma raised her brows. "But I'm working on base."

"As a civilian. You shouldn't let all that military bull bother you anymore."

Karine didn't get it. Civilians didn't get the strange way of life in the military even when she'd tried to explain it. She couldn't relate to the uncomfortable microscope Emma had lived under either surrounded by guys fueled by ego and testosterone.

"Even so, it's a job, so I will remain professional," Emma added. "That means I will not be sleeping with this Marine."

"Ooh, a Marine," Karine said with delight. "Is he hot?"

Emma squirmed as she pictured Vince and his deep gaze, smoldering, like he could undress her with a glance alone. She stared at the cupcake, picked the damn thing up, and took a small bite. Devil's food, her favorite. The sweetness on her tongue made her moan. "Yes."

"Was the sex good?" Karine prodded.

Emma was on her second bite, much bigger this time. She swallowed. "Very hot."

Karine clapped her hands together. "Damn. And you kept this from me all this time? I'm a married mom of a toddler. You've gotta give me the juicy stories. My sex life has slowed to the speed of an old lady driving in the slow lane on a Sunday."

Emma laughed about the situation for the first time. "That was part of the reason why. You were dealing with a baby and keeping your business going. I didn't want to bother you with my silly problems."

Karine gestured with a circular wave. "Please. We're friends. And why call that a problem? If you had a good time, good for you."

"Perhaps," Emma conceded. She thought of what they'd done that night, and thinking she'd never see him again had given her a freedom to act without any inhibitions. Heat rose in her body and it had little to do with the fact she was standing in a kitchen with the oven on.

She took another bite of the cupcake. "Still, I just want to get the next few days over with so I can put that situation behind me for good."

SATURDAY MORNING, EMMA PACED THROUGH THE LIBRARY. Why was she so antsy about seeing him again? She'd taken more care than usual with her clothing, making sure her slacks and blouse were flattering. She'd chosen a gray pair that made her butt look good and a blue blouse that was a flattering color—it also had a nice cut with the right combo of fit and flair. When she'd applied makeup, she'd added another coat of mascara and gloss.

It's perfectly normal to want to look nice. It has nothing to do with Vince.

Ha, who was she trying to kid? She glanced at the clock yet again, it showed almost nine. He'd arrive any minute.

She left the library and entered the lecture hall where the conference was being held. Her plan was to stay near plenty of people so they wouldn't have a chance to be alone—which might lead to a conversation that was bound to turn awkward. Within seconds, she resumed pacing.

"You look like you're about to pace a hole through the hardwood floor," a man's voice from behind her said.

When she heard that low croon, her breath hitched. Time to face her past—which had forced its way into her present.

She turned and planted a polite smile. "Staff Sergeant DeMarchis. Thank you for speaking today. I know many people are looking forward to it."

He quirked his brows. "Are you?"

That stare was back and every bit as disarming—with a bit of teasing and whole lot of simmering heat.

"Uh—um—of course." Shit, now she was stammering. "Why wouldn't I be?"

He took in the room with a remnant of a smile still on his face. "Perhaps I did something offensive to make you run off."

Emma stifled a groan. He wasn't going to make it easy, was he? She glanced around to make sure they wouldn't be overheard. Most of the attendees hadn't arrived yet, but staff milled about.

She took his forearm and led them down the corridor back into a more private space off the library, undermining her plan to stay around people.

Touching him had been a bad move, the warmth of his skin searing her with what reminded her of their once shared passion. She released his arm. "Can we not talk about this now?"

"Sure. How about at dinner tonight?"

Her mouth dropped open. "No," she replied with exasperation.

"Why not? Are you seeing someone?"

"No, but still."

"Still, what?"

She raised her chin. "This is merely a professional arrangement." She motioned to the space between them.

"What happened with us last summer didn't feel very professional, in fact, I'd go so far as to say it felt very, *very* personal."

She groaned. "This isn't the time. I'm working."

He pinned her with an intimate look, as if seeing all the secrets she'd buried in a safe space inside. How did he make her feel so—so—exposed?

"All right, Emma." His eyes took on an amused glint. "You pick the time and the place."

CHAPTER THREE

Vince didn't know where the idea to ask Emma out came from. He chalked it up to the irresistible combination of a beautiful woman in a library. One of the recurring fantasies in his mental file started with a prim librarian unfastening her hair from its bun before a wild night. Emma's hair wasn't in a bun, but it was pulled back on the sides. She dressed conservative in gray slacks and a light blue button-down blouse—which he pictured unbuttoning...

"Not going to happen, Romeo," Emma replied.

Shot down, like she'd pushed one of the stacks of books on top of his expectations, although he probably should have expected that. "Why not?"

"I already told you. I don't date guys in the military."

He glanced back toward where people congregated in small groups and then brought his gaze back to her in silent question. "Odd, considering you're surrounded by them."

"Exactly." She raised her chin. "I like this job. I don't want to screw it up with complications."

"Complications," he repeated. Then he teased, "Good. I'm not looking to date, and I don't kiss and tell."

She crossed her arms. "And that especially pertains to Marines."

He covered his chest as if she'd hit him. "Ouch, my pride."

She pursed her lips. "Your egos are legendary, and you know what they say about pride?" She challenged, planting her hands on her hips.

Amused, he took the bait. "What?"

She arched her brows. "Overrated. Leading to a fall. Shall I go on?"

"No, I don't think my ego could take much more of a bruising." He grinned.

She pinned him with a skeptical glare. "Are you messing with me?"

"A little."

"Why?"

"Your assessment might be true for some, but in my field, there's no room for ego when it comes to explosives. Only calm and steady precision."

She appraised him with a slow nod. "I can see that." Her tone softened.

Their eyes remained locked as he attempted to read her. Despite the challenge in her tone, he detected a hint of interest in her gaze.

"Why are you even interested? We already hooked up. You can move on to the next conquest."

"It's not like that, Emma. *I'm* not like that," Vince replied. "You raised some questions and if there's one thing I can't put down, it's a puzzle."

She snorted and broke eye contact. "I'm not a puzzle."

He regarded her with a curious stare. "You're a puzzle to me, a mystery. You left me with questions that night and hearing you swear off all military men, makes me wonder why. Is it only for professional reasons? Or is there something more to it?"

Watching her visibly recoil, he sensed he was on to something. Like he'd landed his first hit while playing Battleship, and there was no way in hell he was going to walk away now. Yet, he better tread carefully.

The question was—what was he hoping to win?

He scanned her again. She was hot, and he was still attracted to her, but something else intrigued him and he couldn't quite figure out what.

She gave him a look of exasperation. "I can't talk about this right now."

"We'll talk later, Emma."

She opened her mouth and then closed it. Without a word, she turned and headed back into the growing crowd.

Vince couldn't take his eyes off her as she strode away. What was it with his interest? They'd had one night together, that should have been the end of it. He took a Jedi mindset when it came to attachment, avoiding it, because in his line of work, he couldn't afford to get close to anyone. It was a no-win situation, and people could get hurt.

Like O'Brien's family.

Vince's ribs tightened over his lungs. He released a shaky breath, forcing himself to relax. Now wasn't the time to let the darkness unravel him. He had to keep it together for his presentation—he sure as hell wouldn't let himself look incompetent in front of Emma.

EMMA

Emma managed to avoid Vince, save for a few times when he caught her eye. She quickly broke it. His eyes were too probing, like he could read her darkest secrets.

It was time to introduce him. She stepped behind the podium and forced away inappropriate thoughts. "Our next guest lecturer is Staff Sergeant Vincenzo DeMarchis, an explosive ordnance disposal technician in the Marine Corps."

As she ran through a quick overview of his accomplishments, she couldn't help but be impressed. He'd served in numerous deployments in Afghanistan as well as other locations in the Middle East. She forced herself to give him the same polite smile as she did to the other speakers and remained nearby as she had for the other presenters. That was her job. It had nothing to do with the attractive Marine who'd ended her dry spell one explosive night—pun intended.

Or how well he filled his uniform with his muscular body.

"One of the issues we face is with homemade explosives," Vince explained, drawing her attention back to the talk. "They can be made from easy-to-acquire components, like hydrogen peroxide or sugar and fertilizer. Creating a device with a timer can be accomplished with an alarm clock, a mousetrap, and other household items."

As Vince worked through his presentation, nothing was boastful. He shared his deep respect for his fellow Marines and the people he met in other countries. He noted different types of pipe bombs, IEDs, and detonators, and how he and his team had dismantled or destroyed many explosives.

"After all you've seen," a man in the crowd asked, "Do you still experience fear when you see an explosive? Or is it more like routine at this point?"

Vince took a few seconds before responding. "Fear is a natural human emotion, and it's impossible not to feel it, but I've learned to shift my focus. Instead of thinking of the potential disastrous consequences if an IED blows up in my hands, I visualize the strategy. It's like analyzing potential moves on a chess board. You think if I do this, will I put myself in a better position or will it leave me exposed? Then I walk myself through the first step and do it and then the next. Walking through each step mentally at the outset helps me move through the task to dismantle it, rather than being distracted or even paralyzed by emotion."

During their encounter at the wedding, she'd considered him a casual fling, and earlier that morning she'd dismissed him as off-limits simply because he was a Marine. She had to admit his intelligence, courage, and humility didn't fit the stereotype she'd painted earlier.

Had she been wrong about him? Making assumptions about someone whom she'd been intimate with, yet knew nothing about?

Wait, what did it matter? Emma rolled on her toes and shifted her gaze from him. He was just part of her job. She'd get this encounter over with and they'd move on with their lives. Even another fling with him was off limits. She knew better by now. Or at least, she should.

Maybe relationships in the military could work for some people, but definitely not for Emma. She'd been burned by men in the military not once but twice, repeating her mother's mistake. Both she and her mother had been devastated by their husbands' infidelities, their marriages had been dismantled just as easily as Vince had described neutralizing an explosive.

Only Emma and her mother had become casualties.

Emma had sworn that Peter had been different.

How naive.

Well, she'd learned. Her father had served in the Army and he'd cheated on her mother. Peter had served in the Navy and he'd cheated on Emma. No need for round three. She'd seen many men in the military cheat on their wives, not that it was always one-sided—some wives had found someone to keep them company while their husbands were deployed too. That was the problem with military life. It took a toll on families. Loneliness rose and trust faltered. Those marriages that survived had to be based on the strongest foundations, something that Emma had never experienced, and she doubted she ever would.

"Did you hear about the bomb threat in Providence last night?"

That question from an older man in the audience pulled her out of her thoughts.

"No, I hadn't," Vince said. "What happened?"

"Someone called in a threat to a hotel. Bomb squad searched but didn't find anything."

Vince nodded, appearing deep in thought. "It's all too easy to call in a threat. I hope that's the end of that."

So did she. Hopefully, it was just someone playing a prank, even thought it was in bad taste.

As Vince continued with his talk, she stole a closer glance at him. Damn, he was attractive, and not just the physical package.

THAT EVENING, EMMA HEADED OVER TO KARINE'S TO BABYSIT.

"Thanks so much for watching Laura." Karine handed Laura over and wiped the wrinkles out of her dark purple dress. "We haven't had a date in forever."

Emma bounced the cute blonde toddler on her hip. "Anytime. We're going to have a great night, aren't we, Laura-belle?"

Laura cooed and grabbed a handful of Emma's hair. She twisted it out of her chubby little fingers.

John came out of the bedroom wearing a button-down shirt and slacks. "Emma, you're a godsend."

She brushed off his praise with a wave. "It's nothing. Go have fun."

Once they left, she sat with Laura and they stacked blocks. When it was her bedtime, Emma read *The Very Hungry Caterpillar*, *The Monster at the End of this Book*, and *Goodnight Moon*. Laura giggled and pointed to the pages.

After she read one more book and settled Laura into her crib, Emma sank onto the couch with a cup of tea. She glanced around their house and an unexpected pang churned inside.

This was the kind of family life she'd envisioned with Peter before it had all fallen apart.

She shoved that thought aside and her mind wandered back to Vince and his deep brown eyes. They had another speaking engagement next Friday with a visit to a local high school. She was driving him, which meant they'd be alone.

CHAPTER FOUR

VINCE

It was a brisk December Sunday afternoon, snow clinging to patches on the ground, as Vince walked to a pub in Newport to meet his older brother Angelo for a beer. Vince zipped his jacket up to cover more of his neck. He wasn't used to the cold after many deployments to the desert, although he wouldn't complain. He'd dreamed of snow during those long, hot days under the desert sun.

Vince entered the pub and chose a high-top table with a window overlooking the harbor and ordered a beer. Little things like this—being able to walk into a pub and order a beer while looking out at the ocean—were one of the many things he'd never take for granted after a decade in the Marines.

Angelo arrived ten minutes later. "Sorry, I couldn't get down sooner." He shrugged. "Hospital schedule."

A former corpsman, Angelo now worked as a paramedic. "Nothing a former SEAL can't handle, right?"

Angelo grinned. "True." He ordered a beer and then turned to Vince. "How's the training going?"

"Eh, you know what it's like—PT, lectures, chow. The only thing that's different is the base."

"At least this one is close to home."

"A perk for sure." He gazed out at the dark water and breathed in the salty air. "Nothing like being home in Newport during the holidays."

"No better time to be here."

"True." He nodded at his brother. "It will be the first one for you and Cate as a married couple. How are you planning on spending it?"

Angelo chuckled. "We have plans—and Ma, as you know, has her own."

"Sounds like Ma."

"I get it," Angelo said. "I'm her only son close to home, so have to expect some smothering."

Vince patted his back. "Thanks for taking it for the team. Don't worry, I'll pick up the slack after training's over."

After this three-week program, Vince was on leave. Christmas and New Year's Eve at home. He couldn't wait.

They ordered buffalo wings and caught up.

"How's married life?"

"Great," Angelo replied, but then his jaw tightened. "This whole civilian thing has been an adjustment, but being with Cate makes it easier."

"Do you regret leaving the Navy?"

Angelo paused and appeared to think. "No, it was time. I'm happy." He leaned back in his chair. "We're happy." He drank some beer. "But I'd be lying if I said that the transition to civilian life isn't rough."

"How so?"

Angelo glanced around the bar before he brought his gaze

back to Vince. "It's just different. It's hard to explain all the nuances. The structure is different, the routine, the mindset."

Vince scanned the room. Many young twenty-somethings gathered in groups, talking and laughing as if they didn't have a care in the world. College kids? Maybe. If Vince had chosen that route rather than enlisting in the Marines, how different would his life be right now?

"What about you?" Angelo raised his chin in question. "Anything else going on in your life?"

Emma crept into Vince's mind, but he shoved thoughts of her aside. "Not much."

After a few minutes, he finally brought up the subject that had been occupying far too much bandwidth in his mind.

"I ran into someone I haven't seen since your wedding."

"Who?" Angelo wiped his fingers on a napkin.

"She worked with the caterer."

Angelo's brows rose. "Oh?"

"We ended up in my room."

"Did you now?" The look Angelo flashed Vince was half-big brother scolding and the other half impressed conspiratorial smile.

"Yep. And I hadn't heard from her since, until I ran into her here at the War College. She works there."

"Interesting." Angelo studied Vince with a keen gaze. "And?"

"And what?"

"And I can tell there's more to it than that."

"She ran out of my room before I woke."

One side of Angelo's mouth curled up into a grin. "What did you do to her to scare her away?"

"Nothing," Vince protested. He took a sip of beer.

"What happened here? Did you talk?"

"Briefly."

"And?" Angelo rolled his hand in encouragement for Vince to continue.

"She turned as white as the Christmas lights." He pointed at one of the many strings hung in the dimly lit bar, giving it a seasonal vibe.

"She was surprised to see you. That makes sense. And then what?"

"Then I found out she was the woman I'd been emailing about this upcoming conference. We hadn't exchanged last names."

"Shit," Angelo laughed. "Talk about awkward."

"I just want to get some answers." Vince took a swig of beer. "I don't get her. Why would she go from hot to as frosty as this beer without any sort of warning signal?"

Angelo laughed. "She's human, not a machine."

Vince grunted. "Much more complicated."

Their wings arrived and Vince was grateful for the distraction. "Smells delicious."

He ate one and savored the spicy flavors, washing it down with the cold beer.

Angelo ate a wing, appearing in thought. After he swallowed, he said, "That's probably the issue."

Vince narrowed his eyes. "That's she's human?"

"Ha. That she's not a machine that you can tinker with. You're so used to taking things apart to figure out how they work. It doesn't work that way with people."

Vince grimaced. That was a complication indeed. He arched one brow. "They could at least come with a user manual."

Angelo raised his index finger. "No such luck, bro. You need to figure things out the old-fashioned way." He pointed at Vince.

Vince stared, waiting for Angelo to finish.

"Con-ver-sa-tion."

Vince hissed. "Tried that. Didn't get far. Any time I tried bringing up what happened, she avoided it."

"There you go." Angelo brushed his hands together.

"With what?"

"She answered you with her evasion. Meaning she doesn't want to talk about it."

Vince waved his hand. "Don't I deserve an explanation?"

"For what? A one-night stand? There is no explanation needed. It was one night."

Vince grunted. "Okay."

"And here you meet on base months later. No wonder she wants to avoid you."

"Meaning?"

"She's on a Navy base with a bunch of guys and is probably hit on constantly. Here you come along, some Marine she slept with months ago. Do you blame her for being uncomfortable?"

Vince exhaled. Angelo had a point. "So, what do I do?"

"Leave her alone."

Not the answer Vince was looking for. "Can't do that."

"Why not?"

"She's driving me to speak at a high school on Friday. As far as I know, it will just be the two of us."

Angelo took a sip of beer and put the glass down. "Go easy on her. Don't be a dick."

"I'm not a dick," Vince protested.

"If you're too pushy, what else would she think?"

Although Vince tried to listen to Angelo and give Emma space, he couldn't stay away. It hadn't taken long for him to find her office.

Tuesday morning, Vince convinced himself that a casual hello with a cup of coffee was reasonable. She sat at her desk piled with textbooks, the top one on military history. As she stared at her monitor, she tapped a finger near her pink lips— pouty, kissable lips. Her hair was pulled into a loose bun with lighter strands dangling down each side, framing her pretty face. His gaze lingered. She appeared like a perfect picture of his librarian fantasy, one that he pinned to his memory to revisit later.

When he approached, she glanced up.

"Good morning, Emma." He offered her the coffee and a small white paper bag. "I'm not sure how you take it so there is cream and sugar in there."

Her eyes widened. "What's this for?"

"To thank you for setting everything up."

She blinked twice. "Oh, you're welcome. Your presentation was well received."

Although he wanted to linger and talk, he forced himself to step back, heeding Angelo's warning Vince gave her a slight nod. "See you on Friday."

"Yes." She glanced at their surroundings. "Want to meet here?"

"Sounds perfect." As he walked away, a strange buzz of excitement hammered through his body.

Three more days.

Those three days crawled by, despite the busy schedule of the training program. Long days of classroom instruction, PT, and homework didn't give him much free time to muse, yet he still found time to think about Emma. He pictured her eyes as she looked at him, the sassiness when they'd spoken, the curves of her body. What was she doing? Knowing she was so close by on base that he could just stroll on over to see her stirred a yearning that was hard to ignore.

Friday morning finally rolled in like a slow-moving wave that grew in intensity before it crashed onto the shore. By then, he was so buzzed with anticipation, as if his veins had been replaced with electrical circuitry.

He paced for fifteen minutes before they were scheduled to meet. When she pulled up in a dark green Nissan, he climbed into the passenger seat. A pop song played, and she turned it down.

She smiled at him. "Good morning."

She wore a gray sweater dress with a lighter gray scarf. The hem edged up over her knees as she sat, exposing a few inches of her legs. He forced himself not to stare.

He raised the paper bag in his hand.

"What is that?"

"Muffins. I would've got cupcakes," he noted with a scratch of his chin. "But these were freshly baked."

"Ah," she nodded in recollection. "A reference to the colossal cupcake incident."

"A confectionery catastrophe." He grinned.

She laughed. Okay, at least he broke the tension that had loomed between them and had kept it light.

"They smell delicious."

They did indeed, filling her car with their appetizing aroma. He'd bought blueberry and apple cinnamon. She chose the blueberry and picked at it while she drove.

He bit the apple muffin, acutely aware of her closeness.

"How long are you in Newport?" she asked.

"Until after the new year. The program I'm in ends next Friday, and then I'm on leave."

"You're spending the holidays here?"

"I better be," he replied. "My parents are here, and I don't make it home for Christmas every year."

"Right here in Newport?"

"Yes. My dad served over thirty years as a Naval officer, and some of it was stationed here. Once he retired, my parents decided to stay here."

She motioned at the ocean view on her left. "Not a bad place to retire. Or live."

"What about you? Do you live here?"

"Yes, just since the spring." She rolled her shoulders back.

"What do you think?" Vince struggled to keep the conversation light and not too personal, although questions swarmed in his brain. What was she like? Why was she here?

"I like it. I wanted to start a new life after I got out of the Navy and this seemed like a good place to do so."

She served in the Navy? Interesting. "How long were you in for?"

"Too long," she replied with a laugh. "Serving time."

He grunted. Anyone who served knew it could feel that way at times. "Where were you stationed?"

"Mostly in Virginia. I was an aviation tech. When I met you, I had recently gotten out after four years and was still adjusting to my new life with the added bonus of some personal issues." Her expression tensed and she exhaled.

"I've heard about the transition to civilian life from my brother, Angelo. He served as a SEAL, but is out now, living in Providence and working as a paramedic. I have no plans to find out what that's like for myself yet."

She tapped her fingers on the steering wheel. "You plan to be a lifer?"

"I'd like to do twenty. I'm past the halfway point."

"It's a tough gig, what you do. When you were talking about what you experienced…" She shook her head. "I can't even imagine."

"I've had my moments, as we all do, but all I ever wanted was to be a Marine. I can't picture myself doing anything else."

She glanced over at him before pulling her eyes back to the road. "Once I had a taste of Navy life, I knew it wasn't for me."

"Meaning?"

She laughed. "Nothing like what the recruiters promised, that's for sure."

"True, true." Recruiters were often known for stretching the truth to reach quotas. "Plus, you had to serve with all those squids," he teased.

"Is that right, jarhead?" She tilted her head.

"Absolutely." He grinned. "Besides my father and my older brother, I have a younger brother, Matty, who's also a SEAL." He raised his hands with mock exasperation. "I'm surrounded by them."

"Oh, poor you." Her playful tone was insincere.

"Funny." He glanced out the window. "You made it out of the Navy but are back on a Navy base."

"As a civilian," she clarified. "Which isn't as bad."

"What didn't you like about the Navy?"

"I've had enough of that lifestyle. I grew up an Army brat. The constant moving, the family upheaval, not staying one place long enough to call home."

He knew that life well, which is why he never planned to have a family while in the military. "I understand that."

Each of them drifted into their own thoughts for a minute or so. She turned the music up a notch, the Foo Fighters' *Learn to Fly*. She stared straight ahead, eyes on the road, saying nothing. Not wanting to think about his past, he brought his thoughts back to their current situation. He was learning more about Emma, but he still didn't understand what had happened that night at the wedding, and he sure as hell wasn't going to leave today without giving it one last shot.

Angelo's warning to drop it and let her be, replayed in Vince's head, but he shoved it aside. She'd been opening up to him. If he kept it light, he might finally get answers.

Once she stopped at a red light, he said, "Watch out," in a lighthearted tone.

She turned to him with a confused glance. "For what?"

"The giant elephant in the backseat." He motioned behind him.

Surprise passed over her face. "Ha ha. The elephant in the room." She shrugged. "I thought you'd finally drop it. What do you want me to say? I freaked out."

"Why?"

She squirmed and sighed. "I was in a bad place."

"Because you just got out the Navy?"

Her lips pressed together tight. "Part of it."

"And?" he pushed.

"Ugh, it was unprofessional then and so is talking about it now. I don't want to dissect my mistakes."

His brows shot up. "You think of it as a mistake?"

"Yes. No." She raised her hands and dropped them to the steering wheel. The light turned green, and she drove. "It's complicated. You wouldn't understand."

"I know I'm just some jarhead," he teased, "but why don't you try me?"

"Vince, please. It was a difficult period in my life. I'm trying to put it behind me and start over. It has nothing to do with you, okay?"

"Okay, but just making sure—I didn't do something to piss you off that night?"

Her cheeks turned pink. "No. God, no. Ah jeez, I never thought you'd even think of it that way. I figured you were a guy who would be happy for the hookup without the morning mess."

He could understand why she'd see it that way. "I'm glad I wasn't a dick."

She shook her head. "Not at all. You were sweet, and charming, and funny."

Funny? That's how people described his younger brother, Matty. People often thought of Vince as the quiet one—reclusive and nerdy. His interests in sci-fi, fantasy, and geek culture didn't help, so hearing her say that felt kind of good.

She cast him an earnest look. "Can we put it behind us and forget it ever happened?"

Vince covered his chest. "Oh, ego blow." He took a deep, exaggerated breath. "A gorgeous woman wants to forget we ever slept together. Was it that cringe-inducing?"

She laughed and playfully punched his bicep. "No, you goof. It was good."

"Just good?" he prodded.

"Pretty good. Better?"

"Not epic? World-shaking? Shag-a-licious?"

She raised her index finger and teased, "You're pushing it, Austin Powers."

He sucked in a breath and pushed his chest out. "If it wasn't any of those, I think I should have a chance to redeem myself."

She arched an eyebrow. "If you're proposing we sleep together minutes after I say let's put it behind us, I'm going to have to warn you, Devil Dog—prepare to be shot down in 3—2—"

"All right, all right, I get it. Fine. No hotel humping this time."

Her eyes widened. "Hotel humping?"

"You don't like that one? How about suite shagging?"

She snorted.

"I'll get there. Wedding wanking—no, that doesn't work. Ah shit, wedding uh-uh—help me out. You're good with alliteration."

Emma released an exaggerated sigh. She pulled into the parking lot of the high school and parked. "Come on, Casanova."

CHAPTER FIVE

EMMA

Emma attempted to ignore the tingling sensation when she picked up Vince on base that morning, as well as ignore how good he looked in uniform. His biceps strained the tan sleeves of his Service Charlies uniform, which showed how fit he was. His face was clean-shaven, enticing her to run her fingers over his smooth jawline.

After he climbed out of her Nissan, she teased, "Ready to face the teenage firing squad?"

"Teenagers." He grinned. "I'd be better off in Afghanistan."

She laughed. "Tough crowd." She touched his bicep. "Thank you for doing this. I'm sure the kids will get a lot out of it."

He glanced down at where her hand was, and she quickly pulled it away. Why did she have to reach out and touch him that way? She could've just said thank you.

When his eyes met hers, they all but twinkled. "I'm happy to do it. A few of them may be considering the military. The more they know, the better able they'll be to make a decision for themselves."

She grunted. "Better than talking to a recruiter."

He chuckled. "Then they'd be signing papers before they'd finished spelling out their names."

Once they were buzzed in and checked in at the main office, Mrs. McDonald, a stout middle-aged teacher with dirty blonde hair, led them into the library. A few dozen kids sat in an informal half circle while others talked in small groups. Many heads turned and their gazes focused on Vince. It was easy to see why—he appeared quite sharp in uniform.

Mrs. McDonald directed, "Take your seats everyone, our guests are here." After everyone was settled into the chairs, she continued. "Welcome Staff Sergeant DeMarchis and Ms. Bradford from the Naval War College in Newport."

Emma stepped up to the podium first and faced the teens. She gave them a quick overview of the War College, geared for her audience. "Think of it as a grad school in the military, but with topics like leadership, strategy, global issues, and military operations. We have year-long programs or short trainings, like the one that Staff Sergeant DeMarchis is in." She wrapped up her intro as she knew they were more interested in the impressive Marine standing at parade rest behind her. "And now, here's Staff Sergeant DeMarchis."

"Thank you, Ms. Bradford." He strode to the podium and gave her a polite smile.

Funny how formal they were being, considering their intimate knowledge of each other. Nope, that wasn't something she'd think about now.

Vince welcomed them with a few questions. "Feel free to raise your hand to ask questions at any time. I want this to be a conversation, not a lecture. Here's a bit of my background. I've served in the Marine Corps for more than ten years. My dad was in the Navy, so I moved often while growing up. When I was around your age, I knew I wanted to enlist in the Marines."

"Why the Marines?" A boy wearing a New England Patriots shirt asked.

"Their values of honor, courage, and commitment spoke to me. It seemed like the right fit."

A girl with long wavy hair raised her hands. "Did you go to boot camp?"

"I did. In Parris Island, South Carolina, which I can tell you was no picnic."

Some boys commented on how they'd seen videos on YouTube and how it looked so tough, they didn't think they could ever do that.

"Many people think that, especially when they are there. You feel like you're alone and question if you've made a mistake. You face some tough challenges and it makes you think. At some point, you realize that most of what's holding you back is mental. If you can get past the voices telling you you're not good enough or fast enough or smart enough, then you're in a better place, able to reach the goals you set for yourself."

Emma watched the kids respond to Vince's words. The way he spoke *to* them and not down to them, drew them in, even those who had appeared completely uninterested at first. When she brought her gaze back to him, she had to admit she was a bit captivated herself. He wasn't cocky and didn't speak with that smug self-assuredness she'd generalized for Marines.

Fortunately, nobody asked if he'd ever killed someone. She guessed Mrs. McDonald had coached them to avoid difficult topics like that.

When they turned to his specific job in the Marines, he noted, "After more training at the Communications-Electronics School in the California desert, I worked in electronics maintenance. You see, when I was a kid and all through high school, I loved to take things apart and see how they worked. It would drive my mother crazy as I took apart just about every electronic in the house—from alarm clocks to speakers—to see what was inside. To keep our household stuff intact, she'd collect discarded or broken electronics from neighbors, giving me more things to tinker with. It was a good fit. But after my first tour over in Afghanistan, I wanted to move into a different role."

All eyes were fixed on Vince, including Emma's.

"The explosive ordnance disposal technicians, or EOD techs, put themselves on the line to keep others safe. They locate explosives or other risks, such as chemical hazards, and dismantle or handle them to make the area safe. It's incredibly dangerous and one of the most stressful jobs in the Marines. I knew it was what I wanted to do, but I couldn't move into that field right away because you need many years of military experience and training before you can even volunteer."

"But you did it?" a girl with her hair pulled into a ponytail asked.

"Eventually, yes."

"You know how to take apart a bomb?" One boy asked.

"After a lot, and I do mean *a lot*, of training, yes."

Several comments with wows and cool followed. Questions continued one after another after that. Vince answered them all the best that he could until the bell rang, and it was time for them to leave.

Emma stared at Vince and bit her lip. Once again, he defied her stereotype for a Marine. Perhaps her thinking that every guy in the military was the same was flawed. Maybe she had been too harsh with her first impression, considering she didn't even know him.

Except what he was like in bed.

Hmm, she wasn't sure what to think about him now. Did it really matter, though? This was the last time she'd see him before they went their own ways.

VINCE

"That wasn't so bad." Vince said after they left the high school and walked to her Nissan.

"It went great," Emma agreed. "They really responded to you. I have seen some speakers who just talk, but don't listen. But you really connected with the kids. Thanks again."

"You're welcome." He climbed in the passenger seat. Once she started driving, a pang hit him. Soon they'd be back on base and go their separate ways. "Are you hungry? We can stop for lunch."

"I should get back to work."

"Don't you take a lunch break?"

She shrugged. "Sure. I usually take a short break."

He grinned. "You can't leave me starving after speaking with the kids. I need something to replenish my energy."

She gave him a pointed glance. "Are you trying to trick me into going out with you or something like that?"

He raised both hands as in surrender. "No tricks. Just lunch. We both need to eat, don't we?"

"Food is fine. I'm hungry. But that's it."

He was smart enough not to push for more since he'd already scored a small victory in convincing her to go to lunch with him. She was clearly guarded, and damn, he didn't blame her. He'd seen how women would have to fend off unwanted attention in the Marines. Instead, he commented on their surroundings, the music, veering away from anything too personal that would trigger her to cancel their lunch plans.

When they entered Newport, he read a sign advertising an upcoming holiday stroll and another on Christmas at the mansions.

"Once you miss Christmas at home, you never take it for granted again."

"True," she agreed. "I missed a couple and understand."

"How will you be celebrating it this year?"

She flinched. Tension took hold of her body, from the way she gripped the steering wheel to the sudden tightness on her face. Interesting. What was that about? Once again, the urge to understand her rose. She loosened her hold with a wiggle of her fingers. "I was invited to my friend, Karine's, to celebrate with her and her family. Karine was the caterer for your brother's wedding. She has a baby girl, so I'll stop by as an unofficial auntie."

He rehearsed what he wanted to say in his head before saying it aloud, so as not to come off as too nosy. "Do you have family nearby?"

"My mom and step-father live in Warwick, but they're snowbirds. They went down to their Florida house earlier this year and invited my brother and his family and me to go."

"Why aren't you going?"

"They're going on one of those family cruises."

"Not a fan of cruises?" He kept his tone light.

She raised her brows. "A cruise with a ton of kids running around? My niece and nephew are crazy excited, but it's not my idea of a relaxing Christmas." Emma took a deep breath and let it out with a measured exhale. "I'm not really looking forward to the holidays this year, just hoping to get beyond it."

He studied her for a couple of seconds, then pulled his gaze away so she wouldn't catch him doing so. If he had the chance to go to Florida with his brothers and parents, he'd jump on the opportunity. They'd goof around unwinding on the attractions. Something must have pained her to want to rush through the holidays.

"Any reason in particular?" he asked, fairly certain she'd tell him to mind his own business.

She kept her eyes fixed on the road ahead. "It's my first Christmas alone after being divorced."

He rehearsed how to reply so he didn't say something

callous. "Ah, that must be tough, not that I have any experience with marriage or divorce."

She rolled her shoulder back. "My ex got someone else pregnant."

"What a dick." He spat that out before he could censure himself. "Is that why you won't date military men?"

They stopped at a red light. Her expression turned bitter. "That's one reason. But I have more issues than the periodicals section at the library." She glanced over at him with a one-sided grin.

He laughed. "I doubt it. You seem like you've got yourself together."

She turned back to the road. "All right, enough of my baggage for now." The light turned green, and she drove them towards the waterfront. "Want to get a quick bite down here?"

"Sure. I've seen enough sand in my lifetime to want to spend as much time soaking up the seaside as possible."

They found a table near an inside window in a pub that had a view of a courtyard garden. Vince ordered a root beer and Emma an iced tea.

While they studied options on the lunch menu, her phone buzzed. She stared at it and furrowed her brows.

"Is something wrong?" he asked.

"One sec, I need to read this."

Her expression turned worried as she read. She put the phone down and raised her eyes to his. "It was a message from my landlord. There's been a few break-ins in the neighborhood, so he reminded me to lock my door and keep an eye out for anything suspicious."

Vince grunted. "It tends to happen more around the holidays." That time of year could be rough for many people. They might steal for quick cash or gifts for presents they couldn't afford. When they were stationed overseas far from home, it could be dark. Dark and lonely.

This sudden tightness in his gut made him uncomfortable and he shifted in the chair. "Is it generally a safe neighborhood?"

She clasped her hands together, wringing them. "As far as I know. I've only lived there since the spring."

Last year, she would've been married. Had she been happy with her ex? Or had her marriage been strained at that point before he knocked someone else up? Asking those questions seemed out of line.

Besides, what was more important at the moment was making sure she was safe. "Do you have a security system?"

She shook her head. "No. Just a deadbolt on my front door. It's just a rental. I don't have much."

"That doesn't matter. It's your space. Your stuff."

"I know—but aren't they crazy complicated and expensive? I can't deal with that."

"You can get a decent setup that's not overly complicated or expensive."

She shrugged. "I'll look into it."

It only took him three seconds before he volunteered. "I can set up something for you."

"What?" She leaned back. "Why would you do that?"

Good question. He didn't know her that well, but here he was offering to install a security system where she lived. Was that odd? Maybe.

He shrugged. "Why not? Just being a decent guy."

She laughed. "Those are hard to come by. You sure there's no ulterior motive?"

"You mentioned the problem with the break-ins and my natural question is whether you have security measures in place."

"Right." Her reply was edged with wariness. "But why would you offer to do the installation. You only have limited free time, so I don't want you wasting it doing something like that for me."

Nothing about spending time with Emma seemed to be a

waste. No point in saying that aloud, though. He'd had to check himself from coming on too strong. Otherwise, she'd just see him as another horny guy on base trying to get with any female who moved. Suggesting *Because I want to spend time with you. And getting an invite into your apartment sounds like a promising start* seemed too creepy.

Their drinks arrived, and the server took their food orders. Fried clams for him and a bowl of clam chowder for her. He took a sip of his root beer. She swirled the ice in her drink and then sipped it.

He leaned back in his chair. "I'm a tech geek. This stuff comes easy to me. I love taking things apart and putting them back together. I can set up something basic and inexpensive, like what I did at my parents' house."

She peered at him as if trying to gauge his sincerity. "Um, yeah, I guess. If it's not too much trouble."

"Nope. Not at all." He gestured with a wave to emphasize that it was no big deal. It wasn't something he'd do for the average stranger, though. "We'll go pick one up tomorrow. Say around ten?"

She blinked a couple of times. "Okay. Thanks, Vince. What can I do to repay you?"

He couldn't keep the image of sexual favors from his mind, which must have been spelled out on his face as he stared at her.

She arched her brows. "No sex."

He laughed. "I didn't say that."

She fixed her gaze on him. "You were thinking it."

"Maybe it crossed my mind, but I wasn't going to suggest it. You can repay me with dinner. How about that?"

Emma leaned back and laughed. "Should have known. A man, a motive. Food's naturally involved—or sex." She lifted her glass and took a sip of her drink. The iced tea left a sheen on her lips. He stared a second too long.

"Vince, we're not going there."

Despite his rationalization that he was taking this action because he was a good guy, Emma calling him out was dead on. Sex had been on his mind pretty much since the first time he spotted her again. How could it not with how great they'd been together? He liked her. He didn't just want to make sure she was safe, he wanted to spend more time with her.

The attraction wasn't something he could ignore. Since she told him it was a no go, he might as well squash that fantasy.

CHAPTER SIX

EMMA

When Emma returned to her apartment building that evening, she searched her surroundings for anything or anyone suspicious before entering. Once inside, she ensured she locked her door. She brewed a mug of Earl Grey tea and settled onto the brown suede sofa that Karine had given her. Emma's one-bedroom place was a hodge-podge of second-hand and thrift store furniture.

She played a rerun of *New Girl* on the TV for background noise and then opened her laptop. After logging into her neighborhood group online, she fell down an internet rabbit hole of reports and speculation about the break-ins. Some of them were bold enough that the criminal slipped into the house while people were home and then escaped without being detected. One family was eating in the dining room and had no idea that a robber had climbed up to their second-floor window, broken in, and got away with some jewelry and cash without making any noise.

She glanced around her living room. It wasn't like she had much of value to make her apartment a good target. After four years in the military, she'd learned to live lightly. And since she and Peter had split what little belongings they had, she had little more than her essentials. If there was anything worth taking, it was what was on her lap and other electronics. She snorted. Anyone targeting her place would find it a sad shakedown.

Still, the idea of anyone creeping around the neighborhood led her to double-check that her pepper spray and baseball bat were in her bedroom. They were.

Emma returned to the discussion online and got sucked into some crime reports. One guy mentioned a bomb threat at a hotel in Providence last weekend. They had evacuated the hotel, but it had turned out to be a hoax. Nothing suspicious was found on site.

That was good news, but what the hell was wrong with people? Who would create a scare like that? She shook her head. Someone who was nuts, probably, or on some weird power trip.

She ended her Friday night watching a romcom and drinking a glass of chardonnay. The wild, exciting life of a twenty-something divorcee.

EMMA TRIED TO IGNORE THE JITTERS WHEN SHE PICKED VINCE UP on base the next morning. She put on a retro playlist and listened to David Bowie's "Let's Dance."

When he climbed in the car she caught a scent of soap. He smelled good. She resisted leaning closer to inhale it more deeply.

He fixed his gaze on her. "Good morning, Emma. Sleep well?"

And that was why her insides fluttered—those eyes. Those intense eyes that appeared to probe her.

"Fine." She broke their gaze and placed her hands back on the steering wheel. "You?"

"I had some sweet dreams." The slight lilt in his tone made her wonder if she'd been part of them.

No need to go there. Why make today anything other than it was meant to be? He was a decent guy doing her a favor, that was all.

"Must have been a sugar rush." She put the car in drive and headed off base.

She tried to stick to that reasoning while they scoured the electronics in the department store.

"This one is top notch, but it's pricey." He moved down the aisle and grew animated as he pointed out different features of other systems. "This one is good for an apartment. Easy installation and monitoring through a smart phone."

"I don't need to know all the features," she said with a laugh. "I trust your judgment."

"Ah, right. I geek out over this stuff." He stared at the last one and pointed at it. "This one."

Once they arrived at her apartment, a one-bedroom unit in a brick apartment complex, a wild edgy sensation inside returned. She hadn't had a man here since she'd moved in.

"My humble, and I do mean humble, abode." She opened the cheery red door and welcomed him in, ignoring the wild rustle of heat that churned in her core.

Vince entered and glanced around, gaze lingering on her open bedroom door. He turned in a semi-circle. "Nice place."

She shrugged. "Thanks." The tiny footprint wasn't amazing, but it was only her. She liked the brightness of the kitchen with natural light cascading over the yellow walls and white cabinets. The exposed brick in the open living space had a rustic appeal. And the bedroom...

No, she shouldn't think about the bedroom while she was

alone with Vince in her apartment. His presence was distracting enough.

He scanned her living room from ceiling to floor. "Where's your internet hookup?"

With the way his follow-up questions focused on wires and power cords, she guessed he looked at her apartment through a far different lens.

"I'll get us something to drink and then leave you alone to do your thing," she said. "Coffee or tea?"

"Coffee, please. Black."

She scampered into the kitchen and took a deep breath. *He's just doing you a favor. No need to feel weird about this.*

Emma prepared the coffee, boiled water for her tea, and then stood nearby, waiting the glacier-slow seconds until the coffeepot gurgled and her kettle screamed that it was ready.

She brewed her Earl Grey tea with a dash of vanilla. The scent of coffee swirled around her as she poured his cup. She brought him coffee and sat on the couch with her tea. He sat a couple of feet away from her, but still it seemed intimate in the small space. How could she not be aware of how close he was?

"It's a great location," Vince pointed out.

She nodded, but her head movement seemed slowed. "That was one of the perks." Her voice sounded higher, strange. Goodness, what was wrong with her—was she being drugged by desire? She adjusted her position.

Vince stared at her. "Is something wrong?"

"No." Her immediate reply didn't help sell that story.

"Are you sure?"

She put the tea down. "I just—it's just—well, I haven't had a man here yet, and I don't know… With our history." She brushed her hair back. "I hear how ridiculous I sound and wish I didn't say anything."

"I get it. I'm not going to make any moves on you, Emma. I'll be done as fast as I can and then be out of your hair."

A pang of disappointment hit her. "No, that's not what I mean." She reached over and placed her hand on his arm. What the hell was wrong with her? "I haven't dated since my divorce —" But, they weren't dating. She pulled her hand back and sat up straight. "Let me start over. Sorry I'm being weird." She took a breath and smiled. "I'm glad you came here today. Thank you."

His stare was back. The one where he searched her eyes, and it leveled her. He swallowed. "You're welcome, Emma."

She exhaled. Time to lighten the tension and not show him any more of the hot mess side of her that he was already far too acquainted with. She tilted her head and smiled. "Besides, after you're done here, I owe you dinner, remember?"

"Do you think I'd forget that?" He gave her a lopsided smile and then took a sip of coffee. "This is good."

After she'd finally gotten the proper sentiments out, she finally relaxed around him. She put some music on shuffle. "She Will Be Loved" from Maroon 5 played, one of her favorite groups. While he worked on setting up the security system, she grabbed her laptop and checked social media. That didn't mean she didn't steal glances of him from behind, gaze dropping to his butt. It looked as hard and sculpted as the rest of him.

She relaxed, settling into more comfort with Vince in her apartment.

Around noon, she made them roast beef and Boursin sandwiches.

He moaned. "You know the way to a man's heart."

Her surprised expression must have tripped him up since he added. "It's just an expression. What I mean is that it's delicious."

"I know." Still, hearing him say that wasn't entirely unpleasant. Not at all.

A short time later, he announced, "All set."

"Oh." She closed her laptop.

"Just need to finish the set up on your phone."

She unlocked it and handed it over. It was odd to trust

someone she barely knew with her personal things like this, but Vince projected a vibe that was more protective than predatory.

He set it up, and they sat together on the couch. With him being even closer this time, she was acutely aware of how their thighs almost touched.

"You can monitor it here." He showed her the screen. "You'll get a notification if it detects someone entering a window, for instance. Emergency services will be notified, and you can open the video view to see the area inside your apartment."

She took the phone and navigated through the options.

"This is great, Vince." She glanced at a clock. "You did that so fast. I thought we'd be here until dinner, but it's so soon after lunch."

"Looks like we have some time to kill."

"Hmm, is there anything you'd like to do while you have the day off?"

"Oh, yeah." He leaned closer. "How do you feel about escape rooms?"

She tapped her thigh. "Never tried one."

"They're fun." He grinned. "Come on. You'll love it."

Fun was one way to describe it. Adrenaline-inducing was another. The clock ticked down. They only had eleven minutes left before Dracula woke and they faced their doom.

Emma's heart pounded as she and Vince worked through clues in the escape room. They were part of a team with strangers and they had to solve this puzzle to escape. Blood rushed through her veins and her pulse thrummed. They had to decipher a code on an old padlock before the vampire woke at sundown!

When they figured it out, she exhaled. "Whew!"

He passed on the next clue to their teammates.

"You're right, this is a blast." She faced him.

"Glad you're having fun." His genuine smile warmed her.

"But I'm glad you didn't pick the diffuse the bomb one. You'd figure it out before any of us could even spell b-o-m-b."

He laughed. "I'm sure it's set up for entertainment rather than reality. I'd ruin it with my comparison to real life and look incompetent."

"We got it!" the dad on their team shouted.

Their team rushed out the room and declared their victory.

She wrapped her arms around Vince. "We did it!" She then kissed him square on his lips. Scorching energy buzzed through her and awareness of his hard chest pressed against her breasts sent a curl of heat into her core.

Vince didn't respond at first. A heartbeat later, he pulled her body closer to his, and kissed her back with more passion. Her heart hammered against his. She wanted to melt against him, but common sense drove her to pull back.

"Sorry, I got carried away with the win." She gazed at the floor as blood rose to her cheeks. The lingering tingles reminded her that the touch was far from innocent.

"You won't hear any complaints from me," he replied.

Why had she done that? Completely uncalled for.

She shrugged with one shoulder and dismissed, "It was just a congratulations."

When she searched for his reaction, his doubtful expression answered for him, yet he didn't call her out. He cocked his head toward where the rest of their teammates were picking through signs. "Come on, let's get some pictures."

As she and Vince each picked out cheesy signs to celebrate their win, her sheepishness over the unexpected kiss retreated. She chose, "Victory is ours!" while he picked "Winner, winner, chicken dinner." Their teammates took photos of them on their phones and they did the same.

She laughed as she browsed through the photos on her

phone and then covered her mouth. "You're such a dork with that sign," she teased.

"Worth it," he said. "It made you laugh."

She hooked her arm through his and led them to the exit. "Chicken for dinner sounds good. Let's eat."

She'd meant the gesture as a friendly one, but the vibrancy of their connection was undeniable. As they walked, she couldn't ignore the simmering heat between them—and after that kiss...

She pulled her arm away to walk with a less intimate distance. If she wanted to resist this attraction, she shouldn't tempt herself by getting too close to him.

Delicious scents enticed them from the restaurants passed. When they reached a sushi bar, they both paused to glance in.

Vince turned to her. "Sushi?"

"Anytime," she agreed. "I love it."

Inside they were seated near an enormous fish tank with massive goldfish, she ordered a glass of plum wine and he chose a Japanese beer. Service was swift and soon they had an array of different types of sushi, white rice, seafood salad, and yakisoba to share.

She took a bite of the seaweed salad and moaned. "So good."

He ate one of the pieces of sushi. "I got hooked on Japanese food when I was stationed over in Okinawa."

"How long were you in Japan?" she asked.

"About a year."

"How did you like it?"

"It was a great experience to live in another culture, especially one that's so different like that of Okinawa. Gives you a broader worldview, you know?"

She frowned. "Okinawa sounds far more exciting than Norfolk, Virginia. Tell me about it?"

While they ate, Vince told her about the beaches and the historical sites he visited—castles and ruins. "The people were so hospitable and friendly. The architecture was impressive, so different from what we're used to. Parts of castle ruins date back a couple of thousand years. And the food." He smacked his lips. "Unbelievable. If I didn't run as much as I did over there, I'd be in trouble."

She could listen to him all night. Not only was he gorgeous, his broad world view and intelligence added to the appeal. Would there be any harm in having a little fling? After all, he wouldn't be around for long.

"You're looking at me oddly," Vince pointed out. "What are you thinking?"

Her cheeks warmed, and she adjusted in her seat. "Just listening. And wondering."

"About what?"

"If we're becoming friends." *And possibly more.*

Nope. Definitely not more. That was impossible for someone with her hang-ups.

"Friends," he repeated. "I'd like that, Emma."

After the server cleared their plates, Vince suggested green tea ice cream for dessert.

"I'm so full but can't resist trying it."

"We'll share a bowl and if we want another, we'll order one."

The server brought over a bowl with two spoons.

She took a bite. As the cool ice cream melted on her tongue, she murmured, "So worth it."

After he ate some, he asked, "Do you know anything about kids?"

What an odd question. She'd been about to take another bite, but paused to answer him. "A little. I have a niece and nephew."

"How old are they?"

"Eight and ten. Why?"

"I need to go to Christmas shopping tomorrow, and I don't know what to get—or where to go. I'm afraid of making disastrous choices."

Her brows lifted to the rafters. "You—someone who remains

calm while dismantling bombs—is afraid of making a disastrous choice when it comes to toy shopping?"

He laughed. "When you put it that way…"

"How old are the kids?"

"Hmm." He leaned back and his gaze drifted off, as if he was trying to pull together the info. "Around eighteen months, three, and six."

"Ah, that's probably easier than shopping for a teen or tween. That's when they start to get picky. You can find recommendations online for those ages."

Vince drank more coffee and then put down his cup. "I was thinking of going shopping here in Newport. It's not something I get to do often."

"Even better." She waved toward the window. "Plenty of shops around here. I found unique gifts for my niece and nephew. Plus, you can shop local to support these businesses."

He nodded as if sold on the idea. "Sounds good. Would you go with me?" He arched a brow. "Since you are already experienced in shopping for kids, you could be my subject matter expert."

She laughed. "Hardly." He had taken her shopping for electronics today, though, and installed it. Picking out presents for kids was fun, right? She'd be helping to bring them a merry Christmas. "Sure."

"Perfect." His smile brightened his eyes. "I'd enjoy it much more with you."

The lingering look he gave her warmed her cheeks and traveled south. Sure, she wanted to spend time with him, but they were just doing so as friends, right?

Maybe they could be friends with benefits…

Was that something she could pull off? If there was anyone she was willing to test that theory out with, it was Vince.

She picked up a sugar packet and twirled her hand, giving

herself something to do with her hands. "Typical guy," she teased. "Nothing like waiting to the last minute."

"Hey, it's not Christmas Eve yet." He raised both hands in protest. "I have time to shop and ship."

She raised a brow in doubt. "Are they family?"

His brows furrowed. "Not technically."

She waited a few seconds for him to elaborate. When he didn't, she prodded, "I can offer better suggestions if I know a little about them."

He tapped his fingers on the table and fixed his gaze on them. "I've lost touch over the past few months and for that, I'm a real shit."

Curiosity rose like the steam from her afternoon cup of Earl Grey tea. Who were these kids? And why was he beating himself up for not knowing more about them?

"Why?"

"Because I used to stay in touch more. Their dad would tell me stories, which made me feel like I knew them more than I actually did. But not anymore."

His voice lowered to a somber tone. Instinct drove her to brace herself for what might be coming.

In a gentle voice, she asked, "What happened?"

Vince stared at the table long enough for her to think he wouldn't answer.

"He was on my team. We deployed many times together, but that's over. O'Brien didn't make it home from the last one." His demeanor darkened and voice turned bitter. "At least not in one piece."

Emma's ribs tightened as the pain in his voice tugged at her. "I'm so sorry, Vince."

He gave her a tight-lipped smile and shrugged. "Like they say, we know what we're getting ourselves into when we sign on the dotted line."

"Still. It doesn't make it any easier."

He swallowed. It appeared as if he was trying to hold strong emotions back. She hadn't served in combat but knew others who had and that it was difficult to discuss. So few could reveal even the basic details of missions turned disastrous.

Should she ask him any more about what had happened? Or would it be like pouring salt on an open wound?

Then again, he'd revealed that much to her, so maybe he was okay with discussing it.

She debated her options about how to respond to his revelation. Maybe a general overview would be best, then he could decide where to go with it. "Were you with him?"

With his gaze once again fixed on the table in between them, he nodded. He picked up the salt shaker and spun it with his fingers, staring intently at the grains within.

"I'm sorry," she repeated. She placed her hand on his, and he stopped fidgeting with the saltshaker.

He stared at their joined hands for a few seconds as intently as he had with the salt. Then he pulled his hand away. "It's not about my loss. It's about the family's. O'Brien had a wife and three kids. It's them I'm worried about. How are they going to go on without a father?"

Her heart panged with empathy. "When did this happen?"

"In March."

She squeezed her eyes shut. That had been a hell month for her too, with the divorce. She took a breath and reopened her eyes. Her emotions had been so raw then, she'd felt so wounded. Time had helped soften the roughest edges. Had it helped Vince with his loss?

"How close were you with his kids?"

"I only saw them a couple of times for brief exchanges. My connection to them was more through O'Brien. He loved to tell stories about what his wife, Lydia, told him about the kids. He was looking forward to going home to them." Vince's jaw tightened. "And it sucks that it's never going to happen."

"I'm sure he would have appreciated you thinking about his family."

Vince shrugged. "What's a few toys?" He shook his head. "Nothing. It doesn't bring their father back. That doesn't undo any of the pain this family has endured by being torn apart, but I don't know what else to do."

"I think it's a lovely gesture, and I'm happy to help out tomorrow."

He raised his eyes to meet hers and something passed between them in that moment. It was as if they saw each other's wounds and understood. How, she didn't know, but it was powerful enough that she had to take a deep breath to steady her emotions.

"Tell me about O'Brien," she suggested in a gentle tone.

Vince broke eye contact and stared off into the distance. His jaw twitched, and she wasn't sure if he would respond.

"He was always smiling and trying to keep people's spirits up, even on the shittiest of days. Upbeat and had a killer sense of humor." Vince's lips twisted into a private grin. "He loved country music and I'd give him shit about it. He'd give it right back saying it was better than the crap I listened to." Vince grunted to himself as if remembering something. "He was solid, dependable, trustworthy and more than anything, he loved being a dad." Vince straightened and leaned back in the chair, bringing his gaze back to her.

She nodded with sympathy. "Sounds like a great guy."

"He was." Vince nodded. "One of the best."

He glanced at her and then reached across the table. He touched her shamrock pendant and peered at it as if it contained an answer to a mystery.

"I wear it for good luck," she said.

He stared for several seconds and then let it go. After a quick exhale, he changed the subject to neutral observations of the restaurant and other diners, an abrupt shift in tone that indicated he'd had enough talking about his loss for one day.

Soon after, they left the restaurant. Both were more reflective, and they didn't say much as she drove. He didn't return to the base though, and instead asked if she could drop him off at his parents' house, also in Newport.

She dropped him off on a tree-lined street full of Capes. His family's was white and had an American flag out front.

"This is where you grew up?"

"For the most part. We spent a lot of time here." He climbed out of the car. "Thanks for the ride, Emma, and for a great day."

She nodded. It was just as terrific for her.

As she drove away, she pictured him as a young kid growing up there, with wide-eyed dreams about the Marines. Had it lived up to his expectations?

He'd already served over ten years and wanted to continue, which likely meant yes. But he also couldn't anticipate the despair of losing a friend. Her heart ached for him and she wished she could do something to alleviate his pain.

EMMA RETURNED TO HER APARTMENT. SHE TOOK OFF HER BRA AS she often did the second she walked through the door if she was alone. She hated them and would rather have the comfort of soft fleece rather than a wired cage. Searching the fridge for something to drink, she grabbed a coconut water. She plopped onto the couch and stared at the security system. With that in place, she felt more secure after hearing about the break-ins.

Had that only been yesterday? So much seemed to have happened since then, namely during the time she'd spent with Vince. That underlying sensual tension wasn't a surprise since that had hovered between them since they'd first met.

After what they'd revealed to each other, their connection

seemed deeper. Was it simply with them letting down their guards enough to become friends?

Or something more?

She shook her head and released a doubtful sound. Even if she got over her hang-ups, he'd be leaving Newport after the new year.

Still, with Vince revealing some of his vulnerability, she couldn't help but wonder—could two wounded souls help each other heal?

Or, were some scars too deep?

And some people too scarred?

CHAPTER SEVEN

VINCE

Vince lay in his old bedroom at his parent's house, opting to stay here for the weekend rather than go back to base. Although it was now a guest room with a queen bed and no longer had his and Matty's twin beds, it still brought back the comfort of a familiar space.

He attempted to read a fantasy novel, but when he read the same page for the third time, he put the book down. The sparks from that short kiss simmered in his brain. She'd written it off as a friendly, celebratory gesture, but it felt like more to him. Was he reading too much into it? Likely.

And then he'd invited her to go shopping with him to buy gifts for O'Brien's kids. Was that odd?

Possibly.

He groaned. Probably.

It had come up at dinner and it hadn't seemed strange at the time.

Only after he had gone home that night did questions creep

in. Why had he told her about O'Brien? It wasn't something he discussed unless he had to as the emotions were still too raw.

Vince pulled up a photo of O'Brien on his phone, one of them at their camp in Afghanistan together, smiling as if they weren't thousands of miles away from home and being targeted. Less than a year later, O'Brien had been torn apart by an IED, leaving his wife a widow and kids without a father.

It was a harsh reminder of why Vince wouldn't get serious with anyone while he served. His MOS was too dangerous. He couldn't start a family when the risk of it being blown apart—literally—was a serious threat to consider.

Vince closed the photo, saving it to its folder like one of the many compartments he'd created in his mind over the years. He played music instead, a darker play list for moods like this. When The Cure's "If Only Tonight We Could Sleep" came on, he stared at the ceiling.

What was Emma doing now? Sleeping? He pictured her lying in bed, her eyes closed and a soft, peaceful expression on her face. What an enjoyable day they'd shared. When he geeked out and dragged her to the escape room, she had as much fun as he did, enough so that she kissed him—and she'd smelled so good. It took all his restraint not to press himself against her and suggest they go someplace where they could be alone.

What was going on between them? He blew out a rough breath. Fuck if he knew.

She'd mentioned being friends. With that underlying sensual tension always simmering between them, was it possible?

He'd fantasized about her almost every night since he'd run into her in Newport.

Not that she seemed on board with that happening, so he might as well forget that.

Despite that sizzling kiss, she'd put him in the friend zone.

. . .

VINCE

WHEN VINCE WOKE BEFORE SUNRISE THE NEXT MORNING, HE tried to shake off last night's brooding. Today, he'd be spending more time with Emma, and he looked forward to that more than he'd anticipated anything in a long time. Since they were going out to do something nice for O'Brien's family, Vince would keep the mood lighter and focus on the positives. He'd store the darker thoughts to a safe place tucked away. He was good at that. His mind was just a more complicated version of a computer with its additional emotions and senses. He could save the files and close them for later retrieval.

In the shower, he took deep meditative breaths to push thoughts of despair to recede. His unit had undergone training to deal with stress, and Vince attempted to follow meditative breathing techniques to help cope. Repeating mantras and the cool water helped him to crawl out before he sank too deep.

He considered not shaving but did so out of habit. Next week though, once leave started, he would relax, and that included no shaving or haircuts.

After some hot brewed coffee and three eggs, Vince asked to borrow his father's car. He didn't have to ask Emma to schlep his sorry ass around town.

"Where are you going?" his father asked, staring up from a paper from under his Navy baseball cap. Old-school, he still subscribed to daily paper delivery.

"To go shopping with a friend."

"Fine. Take care of it." He glanced back to the article.

Vince listened to Nine Inch Nails on the drive over. When *Closer* came on, he had to change it. He didn't need any more reminders of his ache to get closer.

After he reached her apartment and she answered the door, he took a step forward.

"I'm ready to go." Her voice came out a bit breathless.

Right, they were leaving. He almost forgot when he saw her, ready to spend time hanging at her place again.

Her eyes gleamed with a shimmer of excitement.

Ha. He was probably imagining that from wishful thinking.

The soft green sweater highlighted that shade in her eyes, which now looked more hazel than brown. Her hair was down and tousled around her shoulders, looking soft to the touch.

"You look great."

She brushed off his compliment with a casual wave. "Oh, you know, just wearing festive colors for the season." She raised her index finger. "I'll be two seconds. Just need to grab my coat."

He swallowed the disappointment of not being invited in. What was wrong with him? They weren't hanging out at her place; they were going shopping downtown.

She returned seconds later, carrying both a black coat and phone wallet. After putting the phone in the pocket, she put on her coat. As she wrapped it around her, the sweater pulled at her breasts. Shit, he was staring and about to salivate. He dragged his gaze away before she caught him gawking.

She touched her hair. "Good. It isn't still wet."

The image of her in the shower with water cascading down over her naked breasts did nothing to stop his fantasies.

"It is chilly this morning. You might want to wear a hat."

She nodded and smiled. "Good idea. Thanks for looking out for me." She put on a gray winter hat with a white puffy thing on the top. "Do I look ridiculous?"

"I doubt that's possible." He winked. "Cute as hell."

They walked to the car. He opened her door and welcomed her in. "Milady."

"Thanks." She climbed in. "How chivalrous of you. Not what I'd expect from a hard-core Marine."

He arched a brow. "Then you don't know us very well," he teased and closed the door. After he walked over and entered his side, he added, "Chivalry is part of the package."

She grinned. "I didn't think there's room for anything else besides the massive ego."

The good-natured banter was back. He laughed. "It does take up a good amount of space, but we manage to squeeze in some other attributes."

"I'm just teasing. From what I've seen, you're quite humble." She shrugged. "It's refreshing to see that, especially from someone so smart."

Warmth spread through his chest. Her positive assessment meant something. Before he let it go too far, he warned in a playful tone, "Careful or you'll make the ego monster emerge from his cave."

She laughed with a snort and then covered her mouth. "I can't believe you just made me snort laugh!"

Hearing her laugh in any way gave him a strange sense of pleasure and pride. He kept that secret to himself.

Half an hour later, Emma helped him navigate through options in a toy store. It was crowded this close to Christmas, but tolerable.

"These are good for the youngest," she pointed out a display with simple blocks and other toys aimed for twelve months and up. "As they get older, you have more choices and it gets harder, especially if you don't know what they're into."

"Hmm, that's the case here."

"I got my niece and nephew some of these." She brought them to another display. "They're educational, but fun. Never heard any complaints."

Vince examined the options. Science kits, simple engineering ones, chemistry sets, geodes, space systems—all the stuff he was into when he was a kid.

"These are great. O'Brien would probably be into these and might have gotten his kids into them."

"Perfect."

After he chose an age-appropriate kit for each, she nodded. "Good choices."

He paid and turned to her as they exited. "Thanks for coming with me, Emma. Do you have time to go to the bookstore next? I want to pick up some books for them."

"Sure. I wouldn't mind picking up a new book myself. Something to distract me during the holidays."

His brows furrowed. He hated seeing how much it pained her. What could he do to make it easier?

Trying to keep his tone light, he noted, "I'm around and happy to serve as a diversion."

She gave him an odd look as if trying to decipher what he meant. Shit, did that sound like a come on?

With a slow nod, she replied. "I'll keep that in mind." Her neutral tone revealed nothing.

In the bookstore, the clerk helped him pick out some recent popular choices from the children's section. Then he and Emma wandered through the aisles, browsing for something for themselves.

He found the next book in the fantasy series he was reading and added it to his stack. "I love the scent of bookstores." He breathed in the scent. "I'm a total nerd, I admit it."

"Who doesn't love books?" she said.

"My younger brother, Matty, for one. He hates to crack them open. He's much more of a hands-on learner." Vince remembered one of Matty's remarks and smiled. "We give each other a hard time about it. The first thing I do when I move to a new duty station is find the base library. Matty calls it my nerd magnet kicking in."

She laughed. "I might have one of those too, since I love books."

"What do you like to read?"

"All kinds of nonfiction to learn new things, like how to

grow a succulent garden, but I haven't tried yet. And thrillers--I love being on the edge of my seat. What about you?"

"I'm a total geek. Sci-fi and fantasy are a given, but I try to branch out occasionally."

They browsed the aisles, peering at books.

She glanced at him. "You mentioned your older brother before and now Matty. Do you have any other siblings?"

"No, just the two of them. Matty's the youngest and he's the most outgoing, always joking. Angelo, the eldest, takes his big brother role seriously."

"Meaning?"

"He thinks he knows what's best for others. He means well, but it can be a pain in the ass, especially when we were teens and I just wanted to be left alone."

She peered at him. "So you're in the middle?"

One side of his mouth curled up. "That's right, the reclusive middle brother. One who preferred to stay in his room working on projects." He raised his chin. "What about you? You mentioned a brother."

"Right, it's Kyle and me, and he's five years older. With just the two of us, it isn't bad, but I definitely know what you mean about having an older brother who thinks he knows what's best for you."

She spotted a paperback thriller and picked it up. "I've wanted to read this."

"It's on me, to thank you for helping me out today."

Her brows furrowed. "You already promised lunch to thank me."

"Fine. It's an early Christmas present."

She glanced at his book. "Then I'm getting one for you." She offered her book and reached for his. "Deal?"

"Deal." He stared at the book in her hands. A gift from her. Not just a gift, a book. One that would remind him of his time here with her. He always tried to bring a few books with him when he was deployed. They provided an escape when he was far from home. This book would have another meaning—a connection to Emma.

His muscles tensed. Soon after the new year, he would go back to his duty station. Where did that leave them? Would they carry on as friends? Or would she end up being just another person he'd met, part of his life for a brief while and then never seen again? That was common with relationships in the military. You could live and work and breathe with someone for months—and then someone was reassigned. Gone. That was why it was better to avoid attachments, but was it already too late with Emma? Because the more he spent time with her, the more time he wanted to spend with her. At least while he could.

They passed an area with leather armchairs and a portable fireplace.

"One day, I want a reading nook like this. A house with a fireplace and a large bookcase in the living room."

"I hope it's filled with many leather-bound books and smells like rich mahogany," Emma said in a deeper voice.

When he caught on that she was quoting Ron Burgundy from *Anchorman*, he laughed. "Exactly. Thanks for laughing at my dream."

"Not at all." She brushed it off with a wave. "I get it. You get relocated to different locations. It's good to have a symbol of what you want in your mind."

"Do you have one?"

"I did."

"And now?"

She frowned and her gaze drifted. "I don't know."

AFTER THEY LEFT THE STORE, THEY EXCHANGED GIFTS. Light snowflakes had started to fall, but melted on the sidewalk

"It's snowing!" She stuck out her tongue and caught one.

He ignored the stiffness in his groin and followed suit, sticking his tongue out to catch one. "Ready for lunch?"

Once they were seated at a café that served panini and frothy coffees, he continued with their conversation, trying to uncover what she wanted. "What about what you want from life?"

"Oh, that's a big question." She took a sip of coffee and the froth stuck to her lips. When she licked it, he tried to avoid staring at her mouth with the shine on her pink lips.

"The divorce changed everything," she admitted. "I'm creating a new version of my future by starting over."

That made sense. "What are some things you see in this new version?"

She chewed a bite of the sandwich and appeared to contemplate the question. "I'd like to travel more, especially while I'm in my twenties."

"What's stopping you?"

She stared at him and shrugged. "Good question." She glanced away. "The funny thing about starting over is questioning what you always thought you wanted. Is it still the case?"

Vince considered those words. He'd spent his entire military career avoiding getting serious with anyone. But the more he spent time with Emma, the more he questioned if that was still what he wanted.

"I think that's part of getting older," he replied. "With more experience, you better understand who you are."

When she brought her eyes back to meet his, their gazes locked.

His palms heated. "And who you want."

"Who?" she repeated.

Shit, he meant to say *what*. He cleared his throat. "What," he clarified. "What you want."

CHAPTER EIGHT

VINCE

On Monday morning, training resumed. Vince had eaten dinner with his family last night and returned to base. At lunchtime, he wanted to stop by and see Emma, but held himself back. After all, they'd spent the past three days together. He couldn't crowd her, besides, he had packages to send.

The next day, though, he couldn't keep away, and found her cataloging a stack of military history books.

"I thought you might like to know that I shipped off the kids' packages yesterday and they should get there tomorrow."

She grinned. "Glad you didn't wait until the last minute."

"Want to get lunch?" He tried to sound casual.

Her brows furrowed. "I can't today. How about tomorrow?"

"Can't. Training." The next few days of the program he was in would be intense, not leaving much free time. He wouldn't have much of a break until Friday.

Her expression reflected his disappointment. "Another time," she said.

The days dragged by and he texted her when he could. By the time he had a few minutes to stop by her desk on Friday, the yearning had grown uncomfortable. When he saw her again, her dark hair pulled up into a bun with some loose strands falling over her face, he exhaled.

This wasn't good. He shouldn't allow himself to feel this way about her.

Still, he couldn't resist flirting. "Miss me?"

She glanced up. Her surprised expression turned delighted, but then she replaced it with a challenging grin. "Were you gone?"

He grinned. "Don't worry, I'm back." He moved closer, leaning on the edge of her desk. "How was your swim last night?"

"Refreshing."

Over text yesterday, she'd noted that she often worked out on the base gym and was swimming last night. The image of Emma in a swimsuit had done nothing to stifle his near constant thoughts of her.

"Oh, that's good," he noted. "I'm a free man as of sixteen-hundred when I start leave. Want to celebrate with me?"

She bit her lip. "I'd love to, but I promised Karine I'd help. She has so many catering orders this time of year." She shrugged. "Plus, it helps me out with Christmas money."

He covered his heart and stumbled back as if he was shot. "You're blowing me off, aren't you?"

She giggled and touched his hand. "No, Vince. I'm free all day tomorrow. Want to go to the Breakers with me? Do all the Newport holiday stuff?"

The mansion? "I thought you wanted to just get through the holidays and get them over with?"

She shrugged and glanced off into the distance. "Maybe you helped me get more into the spirit when we were shopping."

When her eyes met his, they locked. His heart hammered. In that palpable moment, he'd swear that there was something deeper there connecting them.

This time, he was the one who had to break eye contact. It was too intense. He cleared his throat. "Sure. I haven't been to the mansions since I was in high school. I'll go anywhere you'd like."

"Oh?" Her brow rose with amused speculation.

He swallowed and raised his eyes back to meet hers. "Anywhere," he admitted. "As long as it gives me a chance to spend more time with you."

Her eyes widened in reply. She then brushed his upper arm. "You're such a flirt."

VINCE SPENT FRIDAY NIGHT AT HIS PARENTS. WHEN SATURDAY arrived, jitters left him unable to sit still. What was wrong with him lately? He was as restless as his brother, Matty, who had the energy of a puppy.

His father dropped him off near the Vanderbilt where Vince was meeting Emma. When he spotted her leaning against a boulder, her hair fluttering in the breeze, his breath hitched. An odd sense of lightness followed. After not being able to spend much time with her for days, just knowing they had the entire day together flooded him with relief.

He walked over and attempted for a casual tone to offset the excitement building inside. "How did the catering go last night?"

She tilted her head and smiled, which did more strange things to his buzzing insides. "Mostly desserts, which wasn't so bad."

Emma hooked her arm in his as they lined up in the queue to

enter the restored Vanderbilt mansion, a warm sensation spread through him.

"Thanks for coming with me, Vince."

The gratitude in her warm eyes almost leveled him. He swallowed. "I've been looking forward to it." He left out the part that it had nothing to do with the mansion and everything to do with the company.

The scent of pine and cinnamon welcomed them. Vince stared at the countless Christmas trees twinkling with tiny lights and covered in red bows in the opulent interior. Emma sighed with wonder as they walked arm in arm while she pointed out the remarkable details on the décor.

Although the displays were awe-inspiring, Vince quickly grew more interested in Emma's reaction to them—the marvel in her expression, the twinkle in her eye, the soft "wows."

Vince stopped before one of the many Christmas trees and gaped. It was constructed entirely out of poinsettias. "I can't say I've ever seen a tree like this before."

Emma agreed. "It must have taken so much time to create." She pointed from bottom to top. "How many do you think are on there?"

"At least a hundred."

"Spectacular."

They progressed into the dining room. Massive candelabras with long crimson candles perched on a table set for ten. Each place setting with a number of exquisite china plates with hints of holiday red, a variety of crystal glasses, and ornate silverware.

"My parents put together a delicious Christmas dinner, but our table will never live up to this standard." Vince gestured around the room.

Emma chuckled. They ascended the staircase and entered a room full of gingerbread houses. "Look at these!" Emma marveled at the displays. "Miniature gingerbread house mansions."

Vince bent down and glanced inside one of the rooms. "They've even decorated the furniture inside. The attention to detail on these is unbelievable." He pulled himself upright. "I should suggest this as a new hobby for my dad to keep him busy in retirement."

Emma tilted her head. "Think he'll go for it?"

He grunted. "Who knows? He loves to sail, so he goes a little stir crazy when he's cooped up during the winter. He'll be out on the water as soon as it's mild enough." He cocked his head as an idea came to him. "Maybe you can join us the next time I'm back here on leave."

Her small grin widened, enchanting him. "Maybe."

That one word filled Vince with promise. Maybe the future offered a chance where they would still be a part of each other's lives.

Maybe.

EMMA

Later that evening, Emma walked arm-in-arm with Vince down the hill and over the cobblestone. The twinkle of lights along the wharves and on classic colonials looked like candlelight. They passed a tour with people holding lanterns. The tour guide pointed out some historical highlights of the area.

Vince turned to her. "Want to join them?"

It might help her distract her from her response to Vince.

"No, that's fine." She was enjoying their walk alone together through Newport too much to want to share him with strangers.

We're just friends. Funny how each time she reminded herself of that fact, another part of her piped up that she was full of shit. She'd never felt this attracted to anyone she'd considered a friend.

A brisk breeze rolled off the water, and she shuddered. "Argh, that's cold!"

"Come here." He folded his arms around her, blocking her from the brunt of the wind.

She leaned into his chest. Despite the cool exterior of his coat, she wanted to curl into his body heat. He smelled so good and provided a protective sort of cocoon that she could seek shelter in for a long time.

"You okay, Emma?" His voice caught.

Was he as affected as she was? Aware that the breeze had passed, and she was still pressed against him, she pulled away with reluctance. Being in his arms felt incredible. If just a short embrace affected her that way, what could happen if they didn't pull away?

"Yes, better now. Thanks." She avoided his gaze, sensing he'd read her sordid thoughts. She rubbed her arms, trying to disguise how much she enjoyed being close to him, and sell it as merely seeking warmth.

He wrapped an arm around her. "Let's get you inside and fill you with something to warm you up."

An image of how *he* could warm her up in such a delicious, satisfying way led her to close her eyes and savor the image for a second. What was going on with her? Did all of her thoughts have to go right back to fantasizing about them being in bed?

Still, she snuggled against him as he steered her away from the crowd and into a pub. It smelled like spices.

"It smells good in here. What's that scent?" she asked the server.

"Our special mulled wine for the holidays." He placed a menu with seasonal specials before her.

"Ooh, that sounds perfect." She turned to Vince. "Want to try it?"

"Sure."

The server returned soon after with an oversized mug. She lifted it to her lips and inhaled. "Mmm."

"Smells like Christmas," he agreed.

When she took a sip, the spices mingled on her tongue. "Tastes like it too."

He took a sip. "Good choice."

"What are you doing tomorrow?" she asked, an attempt to divert her thoughts to a friendly conversation.

He sighed. "Headed to Providence with my parents to visit my brother and his wife. They're making dinner. My mother bought us tickets to a Christmas Carol. I'm going to stay the night and come back with Angelo and Catherine on Christmas Eve."

That meant she wouldn't see him for a couple of days. "Oh, that sounds like fun." She attempted to hide her disappointment with a cheerful tone.

After dinner, they wandered into a venue featuring live music. They ordered drinks and gathered around to hear the band cover play pop hits and holiday classics.

The singer encouraged them to join in, and both she and Vince sang along to *Santa Baby*. Although she knew the lyrics, she was far more aware of Vince behind her, singing in his low rumble, his breath warming the back of her ear, making her body turn to hot liquid. How could he make the song sound even more sensual?

He was so close. She wanted to lean back against him, to have him wrap an arm around her like they were together.

She *should* get herself in check.

But she couldn't fight this any longer. She rested her head back on his broad chest. Vince's voice caught in the middle of a line.

She took another step back, pressing her ass against him. Vince's body appeared to harden to steel. He ran one hand down her side and rested it there.

Her heart pounded in her ears, her body was on fire at every spot they touched. As the song ended, she turned over her shoulder. His eyes were dark with desire.

She gulped. "Want to get out of here?"

"Yes." He took her hand and steered her out of the club.

Once they veered over to walk along the waterfront where there were fewer people, he turned to her.

"Emma." His voice came out strangled and he rubbed his jaw as if he didn't know what to say.

The commercial lights twinkled on the water. The breeze felt more refreshing this time as her skin was almost on fire.

She stared up at him, gazing into his intense eyes. "You know my deal, and I know you're leaving. We can be friends." She took a deep breath and exhaled. "But I don't see why friends can't kiss."

Vince's eyes turned as smoldering as dark coals and he seemed to drink her in. His gaze lowered to her lips and he caressed her cheek. "That sounds like a fantastic benefit to our friendship." He moved his thumb lower, rubbing it along her bottom lip. "I've wanted to kiss you again for so long."

She arched up to him and challenged, "Then do it."

He bent his head, and she raised up on her tiptoes to meet him. The lights along the waterfront seemed to blend into the darkness as time slowed and her heart pounded in her ears. All her thoughts were on Vince—his eyes, his lips...

And then her lips finally brushed his. A strange, relieved-sounding gasp escaped her. The heat was just as vibrant as she'd remembered, singeing her with that simmering current. She wrapped her arms around the back of his neck and stepped closer. He enclosed her in his strong arms and she finally melted against his body, the way she'd been longing to do all night.

Vince deepened the kiss, trailing his fingers down along the side of her neck. But then he pulled back.

She stifled a whimper. "What's wrong?"

He glanced back toward the pubs and restaurants. "Too many people around. We should go somewhere more private."

Shit, he was right. She'd lost all sense of their surroundings as she lost herself in the moment.

The words 'my place' hovered at her lips. Even if they could be friends with benefits, that didn't mean they had to jump right into bed together. He was in town for a couple more weeks.

And after a taste tonight, it would give them something to look forward to.

She brushed her clothing down and ran her hands over her hair. "Maybe we should call it a night."

He released a slow exhale. "Of course." He rolled his shoulders back and adjusted his stance. "What are you doing tomorrow?"

"Helping Karine for a bit."

"What about Christmas Eve?"

She bit her bottom lip. "Karine invited me over."

A heated silence pulsed between them.

"Do you want to get together after we meet our family and friend obligations?"

Her eyes widened at this unexpected invitation. "On Christmas Eve?"

"Yeah, why not?"

She shuffled from one foot to the other. "Christmas is a time you spend with loved ones." She shrugged. "We don't know each other that well."

He gazed at her. "The magic of Christmas is that you can spend it with whoever you want."

The urge to invite him back to her place returned. Before she acted on it, she kissed him on the cheek before hailing a cab. "Good night, Vince. I'll talk to you soon."

. . .

Despite Emma's attempts at distraction, she couldn't stop thinking about Vince over the next couple of days. They exchanged a few texts, sharing what they were up to, and each one made her smile.

On Christmas Eve, she went to Karine's and they feasted on a Mediterranean spread with spanakopita, pilaf, hummus, and tabbouleh. When Karine tried to cover up a yawn, Emma read the sign. She helped clean up, so she could get out of their hair and let Karine and John have some rest.

"I'm going to get going," Emma said. "Thanks so much for having me. Everything was delicious." She walked to the coat rack and grabbed her coat.

"So soon?" Karine asked. "You haven't even had any dessert or eggnog."

That was true. Karine was as hospitable as always, but Emma didn't want to intrude on family time. "It's your first Christmas Eve with the three of you. Enjoy your family time."

"Okay. Where are you going to go?"

"Home. I need to get to sleep before Santa comes." She winked. Baby Laura was too young to understand yet.

After she said her goodbye to all, Karine walked Emma to the front door. "You'll be back tomorrow, right?"

"Of course. I'll be back so soon that you won't even realize I was gone."

"Okay. Text me when you get home."

Emma laughed. "You are such a mom."

Karine waved. "I'd worry about you getting home no matter what."

Karine was always looking out for others. Emma bit her lip, contemplating if she should reveal Vince's suggestion. Ah, what the heck, why not? "So, the other day, Vince and I kissed."

"What?" Karine's volume could wake up every baby on the block.

"Shh," Emma said. "It was a kiss, no big deal. We're still just friends."

"Oh." That one syllable held so much skepticism. Emma ignored it.

"He suggested we get together tonight."

Karine arched a brow a significant height. "On Christmas Eve?"

"Exactly."

"Hmm. That seems more than casual." Karine raised her index finger. "But then again, I'm sure you'd enjoy yourself much more than spending time with an overexcited toddler and her tired parents." She raised her chin toward the living room. "I bet John is already asleep on the couch."

Emma laughed. "I'm sure he wakes up for whatever duties you have planned."

Karine grunted. "The parental Christmas duties. Nothing more." She gestured with a circular wave. "What did you say?"

"Nothing really. I said we'd talk soon."

"And…" Karine prodded.

"And what?"

"I can hear the wonder in your voice, see it in your eyes. The whole 'what if I see him tonight' playing out."

Emma waved her hand and attempted to stifle the blush rising in her cheek. "I am not." It was a total lie. How could she not think about Vince and what he was doing? He'd crept into her mind all night.

Karine sighed and glanced at a clock. "It's still early. Not even eight," she added with a lilt in her tone.

Emma hugged her. "I'll see you tomorrow."

"Wait a second." Karine rushed into the kitchen and returned with a brown paper bag decorated with red and green ribbons soon after. "Here take these for later."

"What are they?"

"Cookies. Pop them in the microwave for a few seconds to warm them up."

"Thanks. You spoil me."

Karine planted her hands on her hips. "Someone has to."

When Emma stepped outside, night had fallen and Newport was all lit up. She was glad she chose to walk over despite the brisk air. Newport was magical on Christmas Eve. So many of the houses had twinkling lights brightening the darkness. Others had festive Christmas trees displayed in their front windows. The stars twinkled overhead and even the crescent moon looked like it was part of the holiday lights.

Sure, she was alone this Christmas, but that didn't mean she couldn't enjoy herself. She still had family and good friends and people who cared about her—people who *wouldn't* betray her. Maybe things would be different next Christmas, but she damn well wouldn't allow herself to wallow this Christmas Eve. Peter had taken enough from her. She wouldn't let him take anything else.

Several minutes later, Emma's phone alerted her with a notification that sounded urgent. She pulled it out of her pocket. It was from the security system that Vince had set up warning of a possible intruder.

She checked the camera. Holy shit. A man wearing all black was in her living room.

She gasped. "What the—" A splinter of fear cracked inside her rib cage.

Who the hell was he? What was he doing there? It was impossible to see his face with the mask. He was covered down to black gloves.

Icy fingers seemed to crawl up her spine

Focus, don't freak out.

Right. She rolled her shoulders back and sought the rational next step, which was displayed on her phone. She followed the prompts to report it as an emergency and connected to an operator.

"Someone broke into my apartment and is in there now. I can see him on my phone."

The operator asked questions and assured her someone was on the way.

After she ended the call, Emma's mind fired up, looping with questions. Would they catch the guy? Or would he slip away? Was it the same person who had broken into other homes? It was a good guess.

What would've happened if Vince hadn't installed that security system? Would she have walked into a nightmare? If she entered the apartment while the intruder was still there, would he have hurt her?

What a way to end Christmas Eve.

CHAPTER NINE

VINCE

It was good to be home. Vince put on a Star Wars Christmas sweater that Matty had bought him last year, but he couldn't keep his mind off Emma and their kiss. What was she doing now? Was she still at her friend's? Was she having a good time?

During their traditional Christmas Eve pasta dinner, his father said, "There was another bomb threat in Providence last night."

Catherine gasped. "Where?"

"The mall."

She exchanged a glance with Angelo.

"Not far from us," he said.

"You need to be careful," his mother pointed out, drawing her gaze to each of them.

Vince clenched his jaw. "That's the second I've heard of since I've been home."

"Right. The first one was at a hotel." His father twirled pasta on his fork.

"Did they find anything this time?" Vince asked.

"No. Sounds like another hoax."

"Damn." Angelo leaned back in his chair. "Sounds like someone on a power trip."

"Exactly." Vince tapped the table. "They do it once, don't get caught, and think they can get away with it again and again."

"Hope they smarten up before someone gets hurt," his mother said.

Vince couldn't agree more. Explosives were nothing to joke about let alone mess with. "I should make some calls. See if there's anything I can do to help."

"They're not going to tell you anything, Vincenzo," his father said. "They have their own unit dealing with the situation, and it's an active investigation."

"Still…" Vince squirmed. With his experience, he couldn't just *not* do anything.

His father was right, that's exactly what he had to do. He wasn't part of this unit. In one way, it was just like the Marines. You only knew what your superiors wanted you to know.

Once they exhausted conjecturing on the topic, they moved onto cheerier ones. Angelo told him stories of adjusting to work at the hospital. Catherine mentioned her latest research in neuroscience, seeking how to improve recall in the brain after memory had been impaired. Vince revealed little about his recent work. The last thing he wanted to do was tread around memories bringing him to what happened with O'Brien. Since Vince rarely revealed much, no one expected that from him.

After they ate, he moved into the living room with his parents, Angelo, and his wife Cate. His mother pulled out a trivia game and father poured them glasses of limoncello.

Vince stared around the room. Two couples and him. He

was the fifth wheel, wonderful. The uneven coupling became more pronounced when they divided up teams.

Angelo said, "Ma and Pop, you're not allowed to be on the same team."

"Why not?" His mother gestured with her hand.

"You'll argue the entire time."

"We will not," she replied.

"We absolutely will," his father added.

"Only if you start," she said.

Angelo exchanged a glance with Vince and then turned back to their parents. "See my point."

Numerous suggestions and protests followed.

"Men versus women," his father said. "That's the fairest way."

"How do you figure that?" his mother asked. "It's three versus two."

"You have a neuroscientist on your team. She probably knows more than all of us put together. I'm retired and forget things, so I don't count."

"Don't give me that much credit," Cate said.

They bickered some more, coming up with different variations of dividing the five people in the room into two teams. Poor Cate. Had she already been exposed to their parents' bickering? Yes, she must have; that was the language they spoke.

Worse were the stolen glances between Angelo and Cate. Too bad Matty wasn't here—Vince would have someone to roll his eyes with each time Angelo gave Cate one of those sickening romantic smiles. Vince still couldn't believe Angelo was married. As he studied his older brother, he saw something he hadn't seen in him before. He seemed more at ease. Not as hard with his always having to be in control personality. He appeared —happy.

They finally settled on the teams of men versus women, thereby making the last five minutes of arguing a waste of time. In other words, a typical DeMarchis conversation.

Vince was competitive in trivia, but he couldn't keep his mind on the game. His thoughts wandered to Emma. Somehow, she'd gotten under his skin.

This was bad. Foolish. She had her own life, and he had his. She made it clear that she didn't want a relationship.

Still, a man could dream.

What would it be like if she was here with him and his family? With her military experience, the bickering wouldn't make her flinch. Smack talk was common, giving each other shit was the norm. He pictured what her expression would be like on witnessing the antics of his loud crazy family, and then he pictured himself exchanging a glance with her, like Angelo had with Catherine.

Damn, he was turning as sappy and soft as Angelo. The problem was he didn't even have the girl, only the fantasy.

"Vince, you with us?" Angelo asked.

Vince stared at his brother and blinked. Shit, Angelo had asked him a question and Vince had been daydreaming.

"Yeah, just thinking about something."

"Something—or *someone*?" Angelo asked.

The others snickered and Vince burned at being caught.

"It's all your fault, man." He raised his chin at Angelo. "All your domestic bliss is messing with me."

"Who is she?" his mother asked.

"Never mind." Vince scowled. He shouldn't have said anything.

He kept up with the questions for the rest of the game. No way would he be called out again. Still, Emma stayed on his mind.

She'd said she was going over to Karine's tonight and tomorrow and had turned down his suggestion to get together tonight. He'd call her tomorrow and wish her a Merry Christmas and try not to repeat his idea of getting together.

After all, it would be Christmas. You spent Christmas with the ones you love.

And he wanted to spend it with her.

Shit. That wasn't right. He barely knew her, so this weird connection to her couldn't be classified as love. He dropped his head into his hands. But he was falling for her.

And it could never work.

EMMA

Emma sat up straight on her couch scanning her apartment. Everything looked the same as it had been earlier that day. The police were gone, and the thief was arrested. Still, she couldn't shake the sense of violation. A stranger had been in this room pawing through her things. She shuddered. Not a good time to be alone.

Should she call Karine?

No, of course not. Karine had enough going on with preparations for tomorrow.

Emma glanced at the TV and picked up the remote. What she needed was a distraction.

It wasn't easy. She flipped from channel to channel, searching for something upbeat to catch her interest. Absolutely nothing spooky to set her more on edge.

She opted out of any romantic holiday movies. No way. The last thing she needed was a romance to remind her that she was alone this Christmas.

Twenty minutes later, Emma gave up on channel surfing and left it on *A Christmas* Story. Since she'd seen it at least a dozen times, it didn't matter that she couldn't focus on the storyline.

She stared at her phone. Should she text Vince and tell him what had happened? She could thank him for installing the alarm system. If he hadn't—she swallowed. She couldn't think about the alternatives. If she did, she'd never get to sleep tonight.

No, it was Christmas Eve. She shouldn't bother him.

He had asked to spend some time with her. She'd said no—because—because what?

Emma picked up her phone and stared at Vince's name, one of her most recent texts. Should she?

She shook her head. She was just feeling lonely and scared. Trying to escape emotions by running into the arms of another man was a bad idea.

But they were friends and it was completely normal to text a friend on Christmas Eve.

Hey Vince. How's your night going?

Emma held her breath while she waited. Would he ignore her?

What seemed like eight thousand seconds ticked by but was probably more like eight before she saw the dots flow, indicating he was typing. A strange sensation lit her up like a jolt of fire to her veins.

I feel like the Christmas goose.

She grinned, eager to hear his explanation. *Why is that?*

My mom keeps feeding me. I can't eat another thing.

Same here. Except it was Karine.

Did you have a good night?

Sure. Just hanging out back home now. Thought I'd say Merry Christmas Eve.

Merry Christmas Eve to you too.

She bit her lip. Counted out the seconds. Debated what to do.

Screw it. *Do you want to come over?*

Eight thousand more seconds went by. The dots appeared, indicating he was responding. What was he typing? Why wouldn't it just come through in real time?

Of course. Are you sure?

Oh, thank God. She heaved forward with a huge sigh.

I wouldn't have asked if I didn't mean it. She added a winky emoji. She groaned. "That" could be interpreted in a variety of ways, and the main one that came to mind was sexual. Eek, at least she hadn't sent him the eggplant emoji.

Can I bring anything?

"Don't you dare reply with the eggplant!" she chastised herself aloud.

No. Just you.

She dropped her head back. Why did all her texts come out like she was flirting? Wait, was she? Ugh, she didn't know what she wanted—all she knew was she wanted to see him.

I'll be there soon.

She put down the phone and paced through her living room. She chewed her fingernails, something she only did when her nerves ran rampant. Was this a good idea?

CHAPTER TEN

VINCE

Just you. Emma's text repeated in Vince's head. What did that mean? He carried his empty limoncello glass to the kitchen and put it in the dishwasher.

When he returned to the living room, he asked his father, "Can I use your car?"

"Where are you going?" his mother replied. "Nothing's open tonight."

"To see a friend."

"Friend?" His mother repeated with arched brows. "On Christmas Eve. *She* must be someone special."

She was. But Vince didn't respond. It would lead to a line of questioning that would delay him getting to Emma.

"First, Angelo and Cate leave, and now you?" she protested.

"It's their first Christmas together," his father said. "Of course they want to spend some time alone. And Vincenzo is in his twenties, he has other people to see besides us." He nodded at Vince. "Go, take it."

"Thanks." Vince grabbed his coat and kissed his mom on the cheek on the way out. "You won't even know I'm gone. I'll be up early for Christmas morning."

"Okay, be careful." She hugged him.

About what? After serving in combat on other continents, he'd hardly consider Rhode Island a danger zone. But she was his mom, and she worried about him. She worried about them all.

"I will. See you tomorrow."

He considered changing out of his Christmas sweater, but left it on. He was a geek at heart, and there was no need to hide it. He rushed out of the house before being bombarded by a slew of questions.

Anticipation hammered through him like in the firing of a machine gun as he drove there.

Don't read anything into it. She just wants to hang out.

He played a podcast to distract himself, one that dabbled on many of the topics he loved about geek culture—video games, sci-fi, Comic-Con, and his favorite cult classic *Firefly*. Today, they'd returned to a debate on the latest Star Wars movie, comparing it to the final Harry Potter book. Vince contributed his thoughts out loud as if part of the conversation, although no one would hear him.

After he parked and walked to her brick apartment building, he glanced up at the locations where he'd set up the cameras at all possible entrances into her place and the instinct to care for her rose. She had a second-floor apartment, but that wouldn't prevent someone from accessing the fire escape and finding a way to break in. He rubbed his jaw and tried to snap himself out of reading into things. Maybe installing that system had stirred a duty to protect her.

Damn it, this wasn't a puzzle to be solved.

Vince rang the bell. He rolled on his feet as he waited and counted.

It took seven seconds before she unlocked the door. A lucky number. Shit, he had to shove aside any fantasies of how tonight could play out. He was not getting lucky tonight.

Emma opened the door and smiled. The warmth of her expression hit him square in the chest. He sucked in a breath.

"Come in." She welcomed him into the apartment.

It smelled like cookies and—he inhaled—*her*. An urge to kiss her rose, but he forced himself not to go all alpha male the second he entered her place.

He scanned her from head to foot. She wore a long red cashmere sweater over a pair of black leggings. Both appeared soft and comfortable. Would they be as soft as her skin? "You look beautiful as always." He stepped inside her living room and gave her a chaste kiss on the cheek before he took off his coat.

"Thanks." After she closed the door, she glanced at his Star Wars Christmas sweater and arched a brow. "Festive."

"It was a gift from my brother." He grinned. "I have plenty more shirts declaring my proud geek status."

She laughed. "Good to know." After a few seconds, she bit her lip. "Is it weird inviting you here?"

"Weird how?"

"You know, it being Christmas Eve and all?"

"Not at all. I'm glad you called. My brother and his wife already left. Otherwise I'd just sink into the couch and drink limoncello with my parents while watching the Christmas Story for the 40th time until I dozed off."

"Oh. It's on here too, I'm afraid." She nodded with a sheepish expression toward the TV.

"Here is a different story because it's with you." He took her hand. "Come on." He led her to the couch. "Here comes the triple-dog dare."

She sat next to him. "I've been flipping through channels. Wasn't in the mood for any of those romantic movies like the hot celebrity chef moving into the small town and shaking up the controlled heroine's life."

He laughed. "Sounds like you've seen one or two of those."

Her smile was one-sided. "Not this year."

Vince glanced down. Her thigh was inches from his. He took deep breaths, trying not to focus on her closeness.

He attempted to ignore his awareness of her as they exchanged highlights from their day.

During the next commercial break, Emma stood. "How about some hot chocolate and cookies? I have some candy canes that we can melt in the mugs." Her words came out at a higher pitch and fast? Was she nervous?

He grinned to put her at ease. "I like your version of Christmas Eve."

She bit her bottom lip and turned. As she walked into the kitchen area, his gaze lowered to her ass. Damn, it was perfect. Even the softness of the sweater caressed it gently. Would he ever have the chance to touch her again?

His groin tightened. He adjusted on the couch. Just because she invited him here didn't mean she wanted to sleep with him. He had to stay cool and let her take the lead.

Emma returned a few minutes later and handed him a mug. "Did I miss anything?"

"Not if you've seen the movie already."

She placed her mug on a coaster on the coffee table. "Only about every year since I can remember."

"Then you're good."

He took a sip of the hot chocolate. The chocolate and mint melted on his tongue. "Mmm, this is good."

"I'll be right back with the cookies." Thirty seconds later, she offered him cookies from a plate. The scent of warm chocolate chip cookies made him moan.

He picked one and bit into it. "Delicious."

She placed the plate on the table and took one before sitting back down beside him. Closer this time. Her thigh just inches from his.

"I wish I could take credit for them. It was Karine, of course. All I did was reheat them to make them soft and gooey."

"A job well done." He gave a nod of approval and then grinned.

While they sipped their drinks and ate the cookies, Vince could barely keep his mind on the movie. He hadn't spent a Christmas Eve so warm and cozy like this in a long time. Too often it had been with his team and them trying to summon some holiday cheer a world away from home—or trying to forget it all together.

Would he be pushing his luck if he raised his arm and encouraged her to snuggle against him?

She turned to him. "Did you want a BB gun when you were younger?"

When he spotted the chocolate on her bottom lip, he chuckled.

"What's so funny?" She furrowed her brows.

"You have some chocolate right there." He reached out and wiped the bottom corner of her lip.

Her gaze caught his and her pupils widened. "Oh." She licked her lips.

A moan leaped out of him before he could stifle it.

"What?"

His pulse accelerated to the next level. "You just made it a thousand times harder for me."

Her eyes remained locked on his. "How so?"

He blew out a rough breath. "I've been trying to ignore how close you are and how good you smell."

She opened her mouth as if about to respond, but then bit her bottom lip.

He adjusted on the couch. "I'm trying not to go all caveman and pounce on you but... All I want to do is kiss you again."

She exhaled. "I know what you mean, but…" She crossed and uncrossed her legs. She covered her mouth, but then let her fingers trail down her neck. What was she wrestling with?

Fuck. Had he blown it? Damn, he shouldn't have said anything.

When she turned to him, her eyelids lowered. Her chest rose and fell with quickened breaths. She raised a hand to his cheek and traced along his jawline. She stroked the rough stubble on his face that he'd let grow in. "I like how this feels."

He froze. His body turned as hard as a statue, but one with a heartbeat pounding with desperate anticipation.

Her lips then curled into a smile. "Looks like you have some chocolate there too."

"Where?" His voice came out strangled and he cleared his throat. Did she have any idea of what she was doing to him?

She tapped her index finger onto a chocolate chip on the plate and then dabbed his bottom lip. "Right there." Her voice softened to smooth silk and her gaze lowered to his lips.

She leaned forward in what felt like a thousand ice ages. His body instinctively mirrored hers.

He moved toward her in what seemed like glacier-slow speed.

When his mouth finally met hers, the vibrancy in the connection was palpable. Her lips were soft and sensual, now with the taste of dark, decadent chocolate.

Time still slowed. All he wanted to do was savor this perfect moment.

He wrapped his arms around her and kissed her deeper, and as he leaned her back against the couch, the urgency between them grew. She melted against him, as warm and comforting as Christmas Eve should be.

Vince ran his fingers down over her neck, her collarbone, down to her breasts. She moaned and arched as he thumbed her nipple, drawing it into a hard peak. His cock twitched as he pictured taking that sweet morsel in his mouth.

He settled more of his weight on her, eager to press his erection between her legs.

Emma pulled back with a jerk and squirmed out of his arms. "I'm sorry, I can't do this."

Vince blinked. The sudden absence of her turned into an unexpected emptiness. What the hell just happened?

"Are you okay, Emma?" he straightened.

She sat up straight and dropped her head to her hand. "As much as I want to, Vince…" She sighed. "Not tonight."

"What's wrong?"

She raised her head, and he glanced at her profile. Her slender neck. Then he noticed it—the tightness in her jaw and worried expression.

"Was the kiss a bad idea?" he asked.

"No." She covered her heart. "That was the highlight of my evening."

Vince had never been more confused in his life. "Emma?"

She exhaled and her shoulders sagged. "I shouldn't have dragged you from your family tonight and into my mess."

"What mess?"

She ran her hand over her forehead and through her hair. "When I was walking back from Karine's earlier, I received a notification from the security app on my phone. Someone had broken into my apartment."

"Fuck." His spine straightened as if someone had tied it to a metal rod. He stood and searched around the apartment as if he'd find some perp spying on them or some sign of entry and then returned his eyes back to her. "Are you all right?"

"Vince, I'm fine. They caught the guy." She motioned with her hand. "Please sit and I'll tell you what happened."

It took several seconds before he could release the tautness in his muscles. His blood agitated with an urge to find whoever did this and make him pay. But when he glanced at her and caught the vulnerability in her eyes, all his instincts shifted. He wanted to care for her, protect her. He sat beside her and took her hand. "Are you sure?"

She gave him a one-shouldered shrug. "Okay, I'm a little shaken up, but I'll be all right." She forced a smile. "I feel so much better already with you here."

He blew out a slow breath. "I'm glad you reached out."

With her free hand, she rubbed her eyes. "Let me go back so I don't miss anything. Oh yes. So, I saw this guy wearing all black with a mask and gloves and everything right in here." She pointed in the middle of the living room. "The police came, and they caught him. He admitted to being behind the other break-ins." She gazed at him with appreciation. "He was caught, and it's all because of you. I wanted to call and tell you." She steepled her fingers in front of her face and then lowered them. "But then I remembered it was Christmas Eve and you're on leave and I shouldn't be pulling you into my problems while you're enjoying some well-deserved time with your family."

Blinking through the rage to hunt down the criminal who hurt her, he slowed his quickened breaths to focus on her. "I'd never think of you reaching out to me as a problem. Call me anytime."

"I appreciate that." She rubbed her temples. "While I sat here alone, I couldn't help but think of what could have happened if you hadn't set that up. My mind looped over the different scenarios. I didn't want to be alone." She squirmed. "And maybe I wanted to see you too."

A feeling of lightness spread throughout his chest, piercing the warrior side that thrummed with wanting justice. "I'm glad you did."

"Once you got here, I was so happy to see you, and I didn't want to ruin the moment with the break-in." She chewed her lip. "And then we were having such a great time with the cocoa and movie. When we kissed, it felt so good… But with all that had happened here tonight, I'm still a little freaked out."

Raw emotions warred as the alpha male within itched to punish the man who upset her, but what rose higher was the need to stay and comfort her. "Anybody would be in your situation." He took her hand and gave it a reassuring squeeze.

Her gaze drifted off and then she pulled it back to him. "Thanks for being here for me, Vince."

Before he could stop himself, he admitted, "I wouldn't want to be anywhere else."

His protective instinct took over. All he wanted to do was take away her worries. "Come here," He released her hand and then raised his arm, inviting her to lean against him.

She exhaled and nodded before cuddling against him. With her tucked to his side, he never wanted to move again. How right it felt to care for her.

He held her and stroked her hair. Eventually their attention returned to the movie. Before it ended, Emma's breathing had turned deep and slow. He glanced at her face. Her eyes were closed, expression peaceful and content.

No way would he wake her. He wanted to make sure she rested after what she'd gone through. And damn if he didn't want to stay here and care for her.

Even if he stayed awake and upright all night, it would still be the best Christmas Eve he'd had in a long time.

Spent with the one he loved.

CHAPTER ELEVEN

EMMA

Emma stirred and recognized the familiar dialog from *A Christmas*. When she realized she'd been sleeping against someone, she pulled herself upright. The glow of the television reinforced her guess. She'd fallen asleep in the living room—on Vince.

Vince's eyes were closed, but he opened them. "Hey, you're awake."

"I'm so sorry I pinned you there. That must have been so uncomfortable."

His eyes widened. "With you in my arms? Never."

Heat rose in her cheeks. She remembered the kiss last night before she'd pulled away. Why had she let her damn brain interfere in that delicious moment?

Oh right, because that intruder had broken into her apartment, and she'd been feeling pretty damn violated. Funny, he'd been the reason she'd called Vince over—and the reason she'd backed away.

She glanced at the clock. "It's 2am."

"Merry Christmas." He smiled and it reached his adorable, still sleepy eyes.

"Merry Christmas." She stood and shuffled her feet. She took a shaky breath. "Do you want to come lie down in my room? It will be more comfortable than on the couch."

His eyes brightened, but he said, "I'll be fine out here. As long as you don't mind if I wait until the morning to head home."

"No, of course not." She moved her weight from one foot to the other. "I'd like that."

She entered her room and grabbed a pillow and blanket for him. He was being a perfect gentleman, and yet a part of her wished he wouldn't.

After she gave him the bedding, she said, "Thanks for staying here. I feel better after… you know." She circled her hand, unwilling to state the obvious reason with the break in last night.

"Of course, Emma." He stared at her with earnest eyes. "I'm here if you need me."

She nodded and swallowed before returning to her room. Once she climbed into bed, she pulled the down comforter up to her chin. What would it be like to have Vince here with her, warming her bed? His body pressed to hers?

It didn't have to go far. They could at least keep each other warm and cozy on a winter night.

But, it *could* go further.

That kiss. He was a damn good kisser. Slow and sensual, affecting her in a way that made her body burn and toes curl.

VINCE

When Vince heard his name, he snapped out to full attention. He glanced around a dark room, his eyes adjusting to the dark outlines before he remembered where he was—in Emma's living room. He must have dozed off on Emma's couch.

"Emma?" Was she okay?

She moaned. He jumped up and rushed to her bedroom. The door was partly open, and she lay in bed, hair splayed across the pale green pillowcase. The white blanket covered her breasts, but left her arms and shoulders exposed. Her eyes were closed, and she appeared to be asleep.

"Emma?" He kept his voice low in case she was asleep.

He'd heard her call his name. Was she dreaming?

Dreaming about him?

He stayed and watched, wanting to ensure she was okay.

Her breath came quicker, chest rising and falling beneath the covers. "Yes," she murmured. She turned her head on the pillow. "Just like that." Her voice came out low and sensual.

So fuckin' hot.

Vince covered his mouth, his body turning hot and tight. He'd heard his name when she'd called out, waking him. He was sure of it. That would mean this far-from-innocent sounding dream had to be about him.

What fantasies played out in her mind? A thousand and one came to him, all of which started with him taking two steps forward and going to her on the bed.

He shouldn't…

Now that he knew she was safe, he should walk away and go back to the couch. His feet were sandbags and he couldn't move. He stared at her, transfixed, as her expression softened with pleasure.

Her panting slowed, yet his still came short and ragged. His heart pumped hard as blood throbbed through his body. Every part of him was coiled tight with need.

Soon her chest rose and fell in slower succession as she appeared to fall deeper into sleep. Whatever she'd been dreaming about remained a mystery.

He couldn't stay here and stare at her all night. If she woke and saw him watching her like some creepy stalker, she'd freak out.

She was fine. He didn't have to protect her from any threats. And she sure didn't appear to be inviting him into her bed any time soon. He had to go back and lie down.

Finally, he pried his cemented feet from the floor and walked back to the cold empty couch alone, save for his achingly hard erection.

EMMA

When sunlight filtered into Emma's bedroom, she practically bolted up. Vince stayed over because of an intruder. They'd kissed. She pressed her fingers to her lips. What a kiss it was…

She'd fallen asleep on him and then invited him to sleep in her room, but he'd been a gentleman and stayed on her sofa. The sensual dreams that followed were far from innocent. Her cheeks burned as erotic images flashed in her mind.

It was just a dream.

Still, what a crazy night.

She quickly dressed in a pair of leggings and long blue pullover and stepped with bare feet out into the living room.

He was sitting on her couch, wearing the same clothes as last night and scrolling through his phone.

"Hey," she said sheepishly.

"Morning." He cocked his head as he perused her with a lingering glance. "How did you sleep?"

She shrugged. "Not bad. You?"

"I'm glad you got some sleep." He stood and walked over to her. "If you're feeling okay, I'm going to head home."

She nodded. "Sure." She glanced into the kitchen. "You sure you don't want to stay for breakfast?"

He grinned. "I'm sure I'll eat plenty today."

"Okay." She swallowed that bit of disappointment. "Merry Christmas, Vince. Thanks for coming over last night."

He kissed her on the top of her head. "Merry Christmas, Emma. I'll call you later."

A *chaste* kiss. A weight of disappointment settled in her gut. "Okay."

As he walked out her front door, he added, "Text me if anything comes up." He fixed his eyes on her. "Anything."

"Will do." She stared at his retreating body and frowned. He closed the door behind him, and her apartment immediately felt colder, emptier without him in it.

She stepped into the kitchen to make some coffee and sighed. Whatever was going on between them was definitely turning murky, complicated by her struggle between what she wanted and what was the safest option for her heart.

"Merry Christmas!" Karine bear-hugged Emma when she arrived that afternoon with a bottle of wine and a bag of presents.

"Merry Christmas." The scent of turkey and other baked vegetables reached Emma's nose. "Smells delicious in here."

"You look great."

Emma glanced down at her red cashmere sweater and black pants and then at Karine, who wore an emerald green shirt and a festive scarf with bells. "Thanks, so do you." She turned to the small group of relatives who'd arrived. "Merry Christmas, everyone."

"Hope you brought an appetite. We have so much food!" Karine raised her hands and led the way into the living room.

"Of course. When you're cooking, I'm not going to spoil my appetite."

Emma glanced at the vivid scene. Colorful lights blinking on the tree, toddler toys strewn across the oriental rug, and a toddler entranced by the wrapping paper she crumbled in her tiny hands.

"It looks like Santa's workshop in here."

John nodded. "Santa came last night and brought all these presents for Laura."

"I hope you left him milk and cookies." Emma arched her brows.

"Oh yes," Karine grinned and rubbed her stomach. "They were gone this morning, barely a crumb in sight."

Emma gave Laura her gift bag. She pulled out the books and toys before returning her attention to the shiny gift wrap.

"I don't know why we bothered buying anything." Karine laughed. "She's more interested in the bows and paper. If we just wrapped up boxes, she would have been just as happy—and we would've saved a lot of money."

John and Karine pointed out some of Laura's gifts that they were especially proud of. It might as well have been the set for a holiday movie.

Emma glanced at Karine and John. Karine tended to be exuberant and sometimes overbearing, while John was more introverted and mellow. Even though they were opposites, they worked. John softened Karine's anxieties, and she introduced him to new experiences. They were perfect for each other, and now they moved onto another phase of their marriage by starting a family.

The same as Peter and his now very pregnant wife.

Emma swallowed the sudden sour taste in her mouth.

Peter had broken their vows and with it her heart, yet he started a new story with a happily ever after. How was that right?

Enough of that. Emma had spent too much time trying to understand what had gone wrong in their marriage. She couldn't dwell in the past, especially on Christmas day.

Funny, she'd just wanted to rush through the holidays, But,

with Vince last night, even after the break in, it wasn't a bad evening at all. They'd had hot chocolate and cookies, watched her favorite Christmas movie.

And kissed...

Emma touched her fingers to her lips.

Throughout the next hour, Karine and John's relatives arrived. More greetings followed with more hugs and Christmas greetings. They all settled around the dining room table set with Karine's grandmother's china plates and crystal glasses. John carved the turkey.

Emma kept up the talk with family members. Although a part of her felt like an outsider, Karine was like a sister to her, so she made her feel welcome. But, she didn't know them well. After she'd filled her belly with pumpkin pie, she thanked Karine and John and said goodbye to everyone.

"You're not leaving already, are you?" Karine followed her to the door.

Emma smiled to herself. That was so Karine. She loved having company and would practically force the visitors to move in.

"It's been a long day, and I was up late."

"I was going to say you looked a little tired, but I don't want to be rude. You didn't get much sleep last night?"

Emma raised her brows. "Well, I had a visitor." She'd tell Karine about the break in tomorrow but wouldn't let her worry tonight. She might insist that Emma stay over, but she just wanted to sleep in her own bed and give them space.

Karine's eyes widened. She opened the door and let them outside and then closed it behind them. "Spill."

"Vince came over, and we watched a movie." When she pictured the kiss, she couldn't help but grin. "And kissed." Before Karine hollered with excitement, Emma added, "It was brief."

Karine's eyes sparkled with a knowing glint.

"And no, before you ask, we did not sleep together."

"Still, that's something." Karine rolled one shoulder in a semi-shrug.

"We're still just friends."

Karine crossed her arms and arched her brows. "Are you sure about that?"

Emma cocked her head. "Of course. He's only in town for a short while."

"Are you saying it's like two ships passing in the night while he's in town?"

Emma bit her lip as she thought about it. "Maybe."

"How much longer is he in Newport?"

"'Til after the New Year."

Karine grinned with mischievousness worthy of the Cheshire cat. "Then you have time to steer your ship around for another passing."

Emma laughed. "I don't know. It might have been a bad idea to kiss on Christmas Eve."

"Why?"

Emma shrugged. "It puts more weight on it. You don't just make out with anyone on Christmas Eve—it should be someone special."

Karine gave a mock innocent shrug. "Maybe it was."

Emma crossed her arms. "Let's not go there."

VINCE

Vince stared at the puzzle piece in his hand for where it fit in the mystery puzzle. His mother had brought it out after they'd exchanged gifts after Christmas dinner. He wore a new Christmas sweater, this one with a Lord of the Rings theme.

They'd played Scrabble earlier that afternoon and now Vince, Angelo, and Catherine sat around the coffee table in the living room attempting to tackle the challenge.

VINCE

He put down the piece and exhaled. It was his third attempt to find a connection and his third time failing.

If he thought Emma was on his mind too often yesterday, then he didn't know what to call the restlessness in his brain today. Everything that had happened last night replayed in his head—the good with her nestled against him, the exquisite during the moment they'd kissed again, and the outrage when he'd learned that someone had broken into her apartment.

"I've never seen you give up on a puzzle before," Angelo noted from across the coffee table. He and Catherine sat cozy beside each other working on the opposite side.

"I'm not giving up." Vince gritted his teeth.

"Usually, you tackle it with laser focus," Angelo pointed out. "Nothing and no one can pull you away until it's done."

His mother walked in with a plate of desserts and stared at Vince. "Oh, now I know something's going on." She put the plate on the end of the coffee table and sat down on her favorite blue armchair.

"What are you talking about?" Vince asked.

"You leaned back in your chair like that." She motioned at him. "Not hunched over the puzzle."

What the hell was up with his family and the puzzle? "Can't I take a break?"

"That's not how you usually act." She pointed to the plate of cannoli and baklava, reflective of her Italian and Armenian roots. "There's dessert."

As if he couldn't see them. He grinned to himself, that was definitely his mother. Next, she would insist that he eat.

"We knew you were distracted by something, or someone." Angelo reached for a cannoli. "And figured if you couldn't focus on a puzzle, then something is definitely wrong."

"You're playing me?" Vince glared at his older brother.

Catherine rubbed Angelo's bicep. "Don't misread it, Vince. He did it because he cares about you."

Vince scowled and stared down at the puzzle to avoid saying something nasty to any of his family on Christmas. He didn't need anyone explaining how Angelo could be intrusive, sticking his nose in Vince's business. He had a lifetime of experiencing it.

His father walked in, carrying a cup of coffee. "Coffee's made." He sat down on his recliner and helped himself to a piece of baklava. "Add a little Kahlua, gives it a nice kick." He took a bite of the dessert. As he chewed, he stared at the puzzle and then Vince. "So something is up."

"It's a puzzle." Vince threw his hands up in the air. "Why is everyone being so weird about this? It's not a big deal."

His mother pinned him with her mom gaze. "Vincenzo, what's going on? Something was on your mind last night and you're even more distant today."

He gritted his teeth. No way was his family going to drop it. "Fine." He ran his hand over his forehead. "I met someone."

She threw her hands up. "Finally, you admit it."

Angelo grunted. Catherine smiled.

"Who else could get you rattled up like this, but a woman?" His mother nodded. "And have you run out on Christmas Eve?"

Vince rolled his head to each side and cracked his neck. "I could've been meeting friends for a drink."

"No. We're not buying that." She leaned forward, eyes wide with speculation. "Tell us about what's going on."

Vince groaned. "I can't figure it out. I haven't been able to since I met her at their wedding." He motioned at Angelo and Catherine.

His mother's mouth dropped open. "You've known her for six months?" She planted her hands on her hips. "Why haven't I heard anything until now?"

That was hardly something new. Vince kept his personal matters to himself. For him to even reveal this much about a woman was proof that Emma had crawled under his skin, making him act in a way that wasn't his usual modus operandi, and according to his peculiar family, affect his skills as a puzzle enthusiast.

"We're not together. I ran into her again here in Newport, and we've spent some time together. I can't stop thinking about her, and I sure as hell can't stay away."

"How does she feel about you?" Catherine tilted her head.

Vince shrugged. "She sees me as a friend. Maybe a little more. She called me to come over last night. But I don't know if it was because she wanted to see me or if she was just spooked."

"About?" Angelo prompted.

Vince summed up what had happened with the break-in and the arrest. "She only called me because she was scared."

"But she called *you*. That means something." His mother raised her index finger. "Who you go to in situations like that means a lot."

True. Could there be something with that? Or was it just because he had been the one to install the alarm?

"I don't know what to think." He shook his head. "Am I being a fool pining for someone I can never have?" He rubbed the stubble along his jawline. Since that invoked a memory of Emma touching it and noting she liked it before they'd kissed, it didn't help matters. He dropped his hand to his side.

His parents exchanged a glance. Angelo and Catherine did as well. Damn couples and their secret language.

"It's the ones who make you work hard that are often those who are worth it." His father raised his dessert fork. "Right, Marissa?"

His mother smiled and nodded. "Absolutely."

Vince picked up a cannoli and raised it to his lips. Were they right? He thought while he chewed.

What he wanted was to hear her voice. Before he was halfway through the dessert, he gave up on it and lowered the cannoli onto to a plate. After slipping into his old room for some privacy, he called Emma.

She answered the phone. "Merry Christmas, Vince." Her voice had an edge of breathlessness to it. "How is it?"

Just hearing her provided a balm to the growing agony that had been crawling through him. "Fine. It could be better though."

"Oh, how so?"

He paused and then swallowed. "If I spent the rest of it with you."

Fuck. The desperation rang clear in his voice, but he couldn't mask it. He had to see her.

One heartbeat. Two. Three. Four. Five...

Shit. He took a deep breath, shielding himself for the rejection.

"Come over."

CHAPTER TWELVE

EMMA

Emma paced through her living room and rubbed her lower lip. When she heard his husky tone, almost a plea to see her, every ounce of restraint in her body yielded. Her invitation sounded as strangled with need as his half-request.

Was it a crazy idea? She stood in the same room where a stranger had violated her space the night before, but then Vince had come over and had chased her fears away. So much so that she'd felt relaxed enough to fall asleep in his arms.

Maybe she was reclaiming her space, replacing what the intruder had taken from her to replace it with a better memory with Vince.

The doorbell rang, and her heart thumped.

She touched her necklace. *Calm down. You're getting worked up over nothing.*

Right, he was there last night, and he was there this morning. She shouldn't feel all these wild sensations zipping through her as if him coming over was something new and exciting.

She opened the door. When she stared into his intense dark eyes, her skin felt so tight and hot.

Exhilarating. That was the only word that came to mind.

"Hi, Vince." Her voice had that higher breathlessness that had come out more and more when she was around him.

"Emma." His was low and throaty. He walked into her apartment and her pulse quickened.

She sensed this was a huge step. As she closed the door, her limbs felt so light and foreign, like she was floating. She turned to him as if caught in slow motion.

He took off his coat and revealed another Christmas sweater, which made her smile.

"Lord of the Rings today?" She arched a brow.

"My family knows me well." He took one step closer to her. "I'm glad you invited me over."

The narrow distance between them pulsed with a vibrant heat.

Her pulse quickened. "I'm glad you came."

Their gazes remained locked for several heart pounding beats. The dark desire in his eyes was unmistakable. This intense Marine with a geeky side did strange things to her, affected her in a way too intense to ignore.

Vince raised a hand and cupped her cheek, searching her eyes. "I've been thinking about you since I left."

She leaned into the warmth of his palm. Her breath rose and fell more rapidly. Had anything ever felt so right?

She swallowed. "I've been thinking about you too."

His gaze traveled to her lips. "What have you been thinking about?" He trailed his fingers over her jaw and over her neck.

His touch and that low velvety murmur all but liquified every bone and muscle inside her. Why was she fighting against anything happening between them? She wanted him, he wanted her. It was pointless to struggle against what they both clearly desired.

VINCE

Emma reached up and touched the stubble growing on his jawline. "I was thinking about how much I liked having you here last night." She swallowed and licked her lips, her gaze moving to his mouth. "And how much I want to do this again."

Rising to her tiptoes, she leaned up closer to him. He bent his head and met her halfway. When their lips touched again, every capillary in her taut body seemed to explode with jubilation, like bubbles bursting forth from an uncorked champagne bottle.

He reached his hand around the back of her neck and cupped it, holding her there as the kiss grew more passionate.

Was this wrong? Stupid? Further complicating her issues?

Screw it, she didn't care. Her world felt right again now that she was kissing Vince, so how could it be a problem?

With his other hand, he stroked along her side. His touch ignited a fire she feared had been snuffed out after Peter's betrayal. Tiny flames seemed to burst through the smoldering ruins of her heartache. Had she simply lay dormant all this time —waiting for the right person to make her feel alive again? To feel like a woman, wanted and desired.

It wasn't the first time Vince had brought that side of her to life. That one night at the hotel had been explosive, but this was different. Back at the wedding, he was just a hot guy for a hook up, a distraction in her screwed-up life. Now he was Vince, the intelligent, considerate, and humble man she was growing close to and it was too much for her to resist. He was as tormented by his past as she was with hers, and that haunted part of him was just as compelling to her troubled soul.

He intensified the kiss, silencing her thoughts. His heat and hardness made her body tingle, and she ached for more.

She led him into her room. Once they entered, her heart pounded harder. She'd imagined him in there with her so many times, and never as much as last night when he was so agonizingly close in her living room.

Having him in there in the flesh outstripped any fantasy. His presence was impossible to ignore. He exuded such a raw, masculine intensity that swallowed all the oxygen in the room, leaving her breath ragged.

"Are you all right?" His tone was gentle, ending with a hint of a rasp that sent a trickle of excitement between her legs.

His concern comforted her. He'd protect her, just as he had since the time he'd installed her alarm and then watched over her last night.

"Yes." She exhaled with a measured breath. "It's a little weird to have you here."

"How so?" His brows furrowed.

She chewed her bottom lip before admitting, "Because I've been fighting with wanting this ever since running into you again."

His eyes widened and then darkened with desire. "Damn, Emma. I've wanted it too—for much longer. I thought about the hot woman I'd spent the night with since my brother's wedding. And then since getting to know you here..." He raised a hand and turned it palm up. "It took all my control to not touch you."

She closed her eyes, picturing that hot night, but then squeezed it away. She was a hot mess then, but now she was in a better place, and she had a better sense of who she was.

Emma ran her fingers along his jaw line and over his sensual lower lip. It was time to forget about the past and any fantasies when the real man was with her now and declared that he wanted her.

"Touch me all you want, Vince."

He lifted his hand to her cheek and caressed her face. The way he looked at her was so intense. Her bottom lip trembled. God, she could melt staring into his dark eyes alone. What he could do to her with just a glance amazed her.

When he followed up with his other hand, cupping her face, she all but ceased to breathe. The way he held her cheeks as he kissed her touched her somewhere deep within, some secret place where she recognized his gesture as protective, sensing he'd defend her from the horror in the world. So comforting.

Maybe she was being foolish considering he'd be gone from her life soon, but tonight she wanted to forget about everything else and just be with him.

He pulled back. "Are you okay, Emma?"

The way he held her gaze captured her in some sort of dream state—one with heightened anticipation.

"Yes. Kiss me again," she pleaded.

He bent down, and she leaned up on her tiptoes. They met in another kiss that seared her down to her feet. He removed one of his hands and trailed his fingers along the side of her neck. Heat traveled beneath her skin. He stroked lower, over her collarbone, down her shoulder, along her side. It was like he was tracing her to memory with his fingertips and igniting a fire that coursed through her body along the way.

She pulled her lips a baby's breath width away. "This feels different from last time."

"How so?" His warm breath mingled with hers as their lips remained close.

That had been a quick and passionate hook up in a hotel room. They hadn't known jack about each other. This time though, he wasn't the hot stranger. He was Vince—caring, intense, and even more passionate.

"More personal. Intense, I guess."

He swallowed. "I know what you mean."

Why was she talking when they could be doing other things? She wrapped her arms around him as they reignited the kiss, running her hands over the muscles in his back. Everything about him spoke of a hardened warrior with a gentle side.

With one hand, he cupped her breast, and she moaned, leaning into his touch. As he slipped his tongue in her mouth and ran his hands over her body, her heartbeat quickened. She clutched at him as they fell back on the bed, gasping for air.

He kissed her neck and nuzzled there. "You smell so good."

"God, I need you, Vince," she murmured.

"I want you too." He kissed his way down the front of her body and then pulled up her sweater. When he touched her bare skin, her body tingled. Wherever he touched her, she smoldered. She reached up so he could remove her top and she fell back onto her bed, panting and waiting.

The dark hunger in Vince's eyes burned like fire in her veins. He lowered his head and kissed and trailed his tongue below her bra. As he traveled down below her belly button, her breath hitched. He unfastened her pants, and she arched her hips, desperate to get them off so he could continue drugging her with this pleasure.

Once he slid them off her feet, he stared at her. "You're so beautiful, Emma."

Wearing just a bra and panties, she felt exposed. She reached for his sweater and pushed it up. "I want to see you too."

He removed it and the Mordor T-shirt beneath and tossed them to the hardwood floor. His muscular chest and chiseled abs were even more carved than she'd remembered. She licked her lips. Delicious. The eagle, globe, and anchor tattoo and barbed wire tattoos were familiar. The shamrock one on his bicep wasn't, but it reminded her of the necklace she wore.

She touched it. "This is new."

When he flinched, the reason became clear.

"O'Brien?"

He glanced away and nodded, jaw clenched.

Wishing she could brush some of his pain away, she ran her hands over his chest with a gentle touch. His muscles were taut with tension. She followed up her soft caresses with soft kisses. The more she touched him, the more she sensed him relax.

Vince pulled her into a deep kiss that sent tingles everywhere. He kissed down her neck and then back up her body. When he reached her breasts, he pulled one of her bra cups down. His warm breath turned her nipples hard and tingling with need. He took one in his mouth.

Eager to feel more of his exquisite mouth on her, she murmured, "Take it off."

She rose a few inches, enough for him to reach behind and unclasp it, and it joined the growing pile of discarded clothing on her floor. He spent time suckling each breast until she was writhing beneath him, hot and wet with need.

He glided down her body, teasing her once again with his hot mouth over her panties. He pulled the top down an inch and kissed the newly exposed skin. Why did they still have clothes keeping them apart? She lifted her hips and helped wiggle out of them and he tossed it to the floor.

She breathed so hot and heavy now, desperate for more. The scent of her desire rose.

He stroked between her folds. "Fuck, you're wet, Emma."

She looked down at him. "I want you."

He dipped his head and kissed her, following with a long, slow brush of his tongue that made her moan. She sank back onto her pillow. He alternated with light touches and longer ones, slowly increasing the pressure. When he added his finger, it added to the sensation. She was lost, absolutely caught under his spell. She clutched at the light blue cotton sheets as he took control of her body.

He owned her. There was no other way to describe his effect on her. No one had sensed exactly what she needed before, not like this. Hell, she wasn't sure she knew until she felt—*this*. He varied slow, deliberate motions with quick, driving ones. He knew when she was on the edge as he'd pull back. The next time, he'd push her a little higher. She hovered on the precipice near delirious and begged for more.

Finally, he drove her to the edge she craved, giving her no

mercy as he pushed her to peak. Incoherent sounds escaped her and then she broke, shattering hard and crying out his name. Wave after wave of intense pleasure flooded through her, leaving her drifting and mindless.

As the pulsing subsided, she reached for him.

He crawled back over her body. "You taste so good. I could do that a hundred times more tonight."

What an enticing offer for another time. "I need you inside me. Now." She fumbled to unfasten his pants.

He stood to remove them, and her gaze followed down the path of every delicious morsel of flesh. When he removed his boxers, his impressive cock sprung out, fully erect.

She bit her lip. God, she wanted him.

He reached for his pants. "Fuck, I better have remembered the condom."

She closed her eyes and grimaced. She might have some old ones buried in her nightstand. She reopened them to see Vince raise one in his hand.

His smile was victorious. "Got one."

"Oh, thank God." She reached for him. "Hurry, Vince."

She sat up and stroked his hard length. He moaned and then tore open the condom before gliding it on.

When he finally covered her body with his, he kissed her and the taste of her on his lips sent a hot coil of heat through her. She wrapped her fingers around his shaft, guiding it between her legs. And then, slowly, slowly, he entered her. Finally.

Shit, she tightened around him. She had to adjust. With deep breaths, she attempted to relax her muscles.

"You okay?"

She nodded. "It's been awhile. Be gentle at first?"

"Of course."

He edged into her slowly until she adjusted to his presence. Once he was fully in, she exhaled. "I'm good."

He moaned. "You feel phenomenal."

With long, slow strokes, he slid in and out of her. Each stroke escalated her pleasure. Their heated bodies were slick. Soon, she clutched him, begging for more. He raised her lower body and drilled into her, each sensation more intense than the previous—too much and yet not enough. She was about to break, but no, not yet...

She wanted to feel more. Feel him from every exquisite angle. "Let me be on top."

"Anytime."

The decadence in his gaze as he watched her straddle him struck a new bolt of desire unfurling in her core. He caressed her breasts and stroked her sides. She leaned forward and slowly glided down on him. This was what she'd wanted and denied herself for weeks—to be with Vince once again.

And even now, she knew in her gut that once would never be enough with him.

She pushed that thought aside and lost herself in this escape, never before feeling so desired. The pressure inside rose. She chased the calling as it pushed her to some wild, unknown destination.

Vince raised his lower body, thrusting harder into her from beneath and driving her higher still.

And then she was there. "Oh God, Vince."

He gripped her hips with rough fingers. "Yeah, Emma. Come on me."

She couldn't think or talk. All she could do was feel. Overwhelming sensations raced through her body sending her over into that secret darkness beyond her reach.

Crashing...

Mind-numbing ecstasy soared through her as she lost control. Quake after quake of pleasure.

"Fuck." Vince throbbed inside her and then pounded harder. Faster. Almost feral. His fingers dug into her hips and he slammed in with one final thrust.

Then he stilled.

She leaned forward, and he pulled her onto him. Their slick bodies touched, frantic hearts pounding.

She closed her eyes and relaxed in the space where his neck and shoulders met as she caught her breath. Such comfort and bliss.

Vince rubbed her back. "This is the best Christmas I can remember."

She'd expected this one to be miserable. It had turned around to be a damn good one and that had everything to do with Vince.

Emma nuzzled against him, drinking in his salty masculine scent. "Unforgettable."

CHAPTER THIRTEEN

VINCE

Back in his parent's living room, Vince sat on the couch and leaned over the coffee table. He attempted the mystery puzzle again on his own, without his nosy family analyzing his mindset.

Not that today was much different from yesterday since he still thought about Emma. What happened last night had changed everything.

Or did it?

What was going on between them was as much of a mystery as the shapes he tried to piece together.

Would he ever understand the full picture?

He had to get out of his head for a while. The best way was with a physical challenge.

He texted Angelo. *Want to run the stairs this morning?*

Sure. Needs to be soon. I'm working this afternoon.

Ah, Right. Angelo's schedule at the hospital was far from 9-

to-5. At least he'd had some time off on Christmas to spend with the family.

An hour?

I'll meet you at the stadium.

Ten hundred was already well into the day for a Marine, which he learned back as an overwhelmed recruit in Parris Island. He'd spent much of the first month questioning if he'd made a mistake by enlisting. Once the initial shock had passed, it became easier to adjust to the routine. They woke early and went for a run, they kept themselves in step with cadence as they marched everywhere together, they ate quickly in the chow hall and had little sleep. All he'd wanted to be was a Marine and that had been his life for the past ten years.

What about the future? Did he have room for more than the Corps in his life, perhaps a version with Emma in it?

Vince finished his last cup of coffee but held off on eating anything heavy until after his workout. No doubt his mother would remind him of the Christmas leftovers every two hours. Which was another reason why he needed to work out.

He got his blood moving with a warmup on the front lawn before jogging to the stadium. A few clouds drifted above in the otherwise sunny day. The brisk winter air kept him from overheating. It felt great. So many of his deployments had sent him to desert locales. The sun could scorch blazing hot on his skin during the day yet leave him frigid as soon as it went down that night. New England was known for its erratic weather patterns, humid one day and snowing the next, but he'd take that inconsistency over those long, cold, lonely nights in the desert.

That situation could happen again any time soon, which increased the yearning to spend another night in Emma's warm bed.

Once Vince reached the football stadium, he scanned the perimeter. Nobody else was brave—or foolish enough to be out here this early at this time of year. He was sure there'd be some diehards burning off their holiday meals the same as he was, but perhaps many were taking it easy during the holiday week.

Running the stairs was one of his favorite workouts back home in Newport. Brutal, for sure. One he'd started during high school football and carried on with his brothers. The climb provided a different type of challenge he liked to conquer.

"You look like you're ready to run away from this," Angelo teased from behind Vince.

He turned to face his brother. "Hell no. I need to counter Ma trying to fatten me up with twenty pounds of pasta flesh."

"Ha, and she's loving every minute of it," Angelo said. "When I first moved back home, she tried to feed me like I'd been starved for the past decade while in the Navy."

"I'm surprised she hasn't convinced you and Catherine to move in."

"No, but she tried to get us there for family dinner twice a week. We agreed to once a week, but I often have to reschedule." Angelo grinned. "The hospital doesn't work around Ma's dinner plans."

Vince laughed. They joked about their mother's fussing, but he loved it. He was sure both Angelo and Matty did too. After being deployed to foreign lands where the enemy sought to take him out, of course he appreciated his mother's care—even when it bordered on smothering.

Angelo said, "You ready to go?"

"Damn straight. I already warmed up by jogging here."

"I better get my blood flowing. Give me a few minutes." Angelo did some jumping jacks followed by high knees. When he did some walking lunges down the field, Vince joined in.

Once they completed the warm-up, Angelo said, "Let's go."

They climbed up to the first set of bleachers. "Alternate stairs and seats?" Angelo suggested.

"Sounds good," Vince agreed.

"Follow my pace. I remember the last time we were here with Matty."

That had been a boneheaded move. Matty had stoked the competitive streak by pushing for a race and the two of them had burned out quickly.

Vince followed Angelo up the set of stairs. He kept it at a relatively slow pace as they worked up for the routine and then descended.

On the next set, Vince led them up the stadium seats, which required more of a lunge. As they alternated through the sections, his heartbeat quickened, and soon a sheen of sweat covered his skin.

They continued in this pattern all the way around the stadium, pausing at times to catch their breath or sip water. By the time they reached the final section, both of them had sweat drenching their T-shirts, despite the winter air. Vince drank almost half the water in his bottle while his heartbeat cooled.

"How did it go last night?" Angelo asked.

Vince's mind instantly snapped back to the moment he'd slipped inside Emma. Her silky heat had tightened around him as she held onto him.

"Good."

"That's it?" Angelo prodded. "After all that anguish yesterday, that's all you're going to say?"

Vince grimaced and rolled his shoulders back. True, it was unlike him to have revealed so much, but he had been tormented by their situation.

And now—had anything changed?

"It was a great night, man. Happy?"

"If you are," Angelo said. "I don't need the details."

"Good, because you're not getting any."

Angelo laughed. "What is up with you lately?"

Good question. The answer most likely had something to do with Emma and wanting to see her again. He'd left right after a quick breakfast this morning. Although he'd told himself it was so he wouldn't push into her space, a part of it was that he needed some distance as well. He sensed himself growing closer to her, and he needed perspective.

Before he'd left, he said he'd talk to her later.

Vince groaned. "Wish I had an answer."

Angelo nodded with an ah-ha kind of expression. "It's obvious by the torment on your face. You want to see her again."

Vince swallowed. As a Marine he should be better trained not to broadcast his feelings. Hell, he'd been damn good at it. But Angelo had known Vince his entire life and could read things that most others would miss.

"I do," Vince admitted. "But I'm debating it."

"About?"

"Whether it would be a bad idea."

"How?"

"Because I spent the last two nights with her."

Angelo arched his brows. "And that's a problem why?"

"I'm leaving next week, and she doesn't want a relationship. So once I leave…" He turned his palms up. The most likely outcome was that this would end.

Wherever he was deployed, would he be haunted by Emma? Remembering the taste of her, the touch of her skin, the sound of her cries?

"How do you feel about that?" Angelo asked.

Vince blinked, staring at his older brother. "Wow, you clearly have been living with a head doctor. Now you're asking about my feelings?"

"Ha, Cate's a neuroscientist, not a shrink. So what is it? What do you want?"

Vince shrugged. That was another good question. "I guess that the best outcome is I walk away. We all know that relationships in the military are hard. And in my field—" He swallowed. O'Brien's wife was a widow and his children were without a father. Vince's ribs tightened. He forced himself to exhale. "We'll each go our own way."

"If that's what you both want." Angelo's tone noted his skepticism. "But I don't think that's the case."

Vince scowled as his brother's words hit too close beneath the surface. "Thank you, Captain Obvious," he teased. "I'm glad I didn't pay money for those words of wisdom."

Angelo chuckled. "Family discount."

EMMA

Emma walked to Karine's catering shop late in the morning to help with a lunch order. Emma had the week off between Christmas and New Year's. Since it was a busy week for Karine and Emma didn't have much going on, she offered to help out when she could.

She couldn't keep a smile from her face when she pictured the night before. It was a cool fifty degrees, but her mood was as bright as the blue skies overhead.

As soon as she pulled open the door to the shop, Karine looked up from behind the dessert-filled counter where she was stirring a wooden spoon with vigor in a stainless steel bowl. "Hey, Emma. You're looking happy this morning."

Emma shrugged. "I had a good night."

Karine paused and arched her brows. "Is there a reason for that smile on your face?"

Emma glanced away, unable to keep the grin from her lips. "Maybe."

"Please tell me this means your dry spell is over?" Karine resumed stirring.

Emma laughed and pulled her gaze to Karine. "Yes, and it was well worth the wait."

"I'm glad to hear that. You're young and beautiful. You

shouldn't let that dumbass-who-should-not-be-named keep you from enjoying your life any longer."

"I don't plan to." Emma stepped behind the counter and washed her hands.

Karine tilted her head. "Interesting."

"What's interesting?"

"Wasn't Vince the last guy you'd been with?"

Yes. Karine called it. It was probably better not to analyze that and add any more questions after last night. "What do you want me to start with?"

Karine directed her to platters of finger sandwiches and deli meats. "Can you wrap those up? And pull together a bag of condiments?"

Emma put an apron on and moved into action. Before she'd even finished wrapping up one platter, Karine asked, "What happens now?"

Emma's shoulders tightened. "Nothing."

"Nothing? What do you mean nothing?"

"Just because we slept together doesn't mean anything has changed."

"Of course it changes things. You've wanted each other since you first met. You may say you're 'friends.'" Karine raised her fingers for air quotes. "But I call bull."

Emma pursed her lips. "Even if we're remotely interested in it being anything more, it can't happen."

"Why not?"

"He's leaving Newport next week. I'm staying here. No point speculating about anything else."

Helping Karine only took a few hours, which meant Emma had the rest of the day to herself. What was Vince doing? When she'd asked him this morning, he joked that he had a date with a puzzle that was giving him a bad rep. He had to claim a victory by the end of the day to reclaim the title of puzzle master in his family.

Should she text him? She pulled out her phone.

No. They'd spent so much time together lately. She put the phone away.

Screw it. She typed *Claim your victory yet?*

Seconds later, he replied. *Barely fifteen minutes ago. It was a tough contender, but I came out on top.*

Congrats! Is a celebration in order?

Yeah. You up for a drink later? Maybe a bite?

Emma stared at the words and her heart thumped. She hadn't technically meant with her, but the wild buzzing sensation through her body indicated her excitement.

Sure.

She dismissed the sudden anticipation that rose with a one-shouldered shrug. What did they have to lose? His time left in Newport was running down, so they might as well enjoy it while it lasted.

CHAPTER FOURTEEN

VINCE

Maybe it was a terrible idea, but Vince couldn't stay away. Spending the evening with Emma was better than strutting around the damn puzzle declaring his victory and having his parents pry about Emma.

Would she let him stay the night again?

A man could hope.

She met him at a Mexican restaurant downtown. When she walked in, wearing a light blue sweater that clung to her with just enough tightness, he inhaled a sharp breath.

When she spotted him, she smiled and walked over.

"You look beautiful. But that's nothing new." He stepped closer, ready to greet her with a kiss on the lips, but he held back.

"Thanks, Vince." Her eyes twinkled. "You're looking pretty good yourself." She rubbed his stubble. "Soon you'll have a full-grown beard."

He laughed. "Which I'll have to shave as soon as I report back to duty."

Her smiled vanished and so did his. Why did he have to bring that up?

He didn't mention his impending departure again while they shared a massive plate of nachos and drinks, yet it hung over them like a storm cloud heavy with rain as though it could come down on them at any moment. What he knew was that he wanted to spend as much time as he could here with Emma.

After they finished up and headed outside, he tried not to sound too eager to head home with her. "It got cold out." The temperature had dropped to the twenties after sundown and the ocean breeze didn't help. "We should go someplace warm."

"Yes." She faced him and their eyes locked.

So much was communicated through that silent connection yet neither of them spoke. She wanted him as he ached for her. The space between them pulsing with a vibrant, palpable strumming convinced him of it. His temperature rose, palms turned hot, and blood stirred through his veins. Had he ever wanted anyone this badly?

Her pupils dilated and her eyelids lowered, framed by her dark lashes. When her lips parted, his heartbeat lurched.

As he stepped closer to her, his movements seemed sluggish and his vision narrowed. All his focus homed in on Emma—her face, her lips, her body. How much he needed her. Now.

He reached for the back of her neck and lowered his head as he pulled them together. When their lips met, the simmering heat turned combustible.

She tasted so good with the hint of the fruity margarita still on her lips. She moaned against his mouth and wrapped her arms around him. He pulled her closer and pressed himself against her, his growing erection straining against his jeans. The urge to be with her again grew agonizing.

She pulled back a breath. "My place?" Her voice was low and throaty.

"Yes."

He hailed a cab to get them there as quickly as possible. While in the back seat, their thighs touched. All he wanted to do was kiss her again, press his body on hers, but it would have to wait. It took all his restraint not to touch her body. Rather than sitting on one of his damn hands, he held one of hers. At least he comforted himself with the heat of her skin.

Stealing hungry glances at each other amplified the sensual tension. The few minute drive stretched out to decades. He forced himself to take slow breaths while staring at the passing scenery outside. The more crowded commercial area shifted into a residential one. Finally, they turned onto Emma's street.

He practically threw the money at the driver when he stopped, leaving a generous tip so he wouldn't have to wait for change.

Emma held his hand as she led the way to the front door, and he followed her, eager to pounce. When she opened the front door, she barely pushed it behind her before his need for her took over. He took her face in his hands and kissed her again, practically plundering her mouth with his aching desire.

He kicked the door closed behind him and fumbled to lock it before he had his hands all over her, touching all the curves that were off-limits to him in public. He could caress her breasts all night, but it wasn't enough—he needed to touch all of her, feel her soft skin. He trailed his fingers down her sides, cupping her round ass. With the way she grabbed at his shirt, pulling it up before she covered his chest with her hands, she was just as desperate for skin-on-skin contact.

They kissed and clutched each other as they tried to move from her living room to her bedroom. He removed his shirt and stripped off hers as they stumbled around an end table. She kicked off her shoes and slid down her pants and kicked them off just after they entered her bedroom.

He stared at her, now only in a lace-trimmed black satin bra and panties, as he removed his shoes, socks, and pants. Her hair was tousled over her shoulders, and a few strands draping on her breasts, which rose and fell with her quickened breaths. Her pouty lips were parted and swollen from his rough kisses. The hottest part of all was the way she looked at him with unmasked desire in her darkened eyes.

"You're so hot, Emma." He rubbed his mouth. "You don't know what you're doing to me."

"Oh?" She quirked a brow.

He took her hand and slid it down over his aching shaft. "Look how hard I am for you."

She gave him a naughty smile as she stroked him with a light touch that drove his need to atmospheric levels.

"Did I do that?" She feigned innocence and surprise. "That's so wrong of me." She then slowly lowered herself to her knees.

He watched in what seemed like slow motion as his heartbeat leaped to the next level. Not only was he back in her room, what he'd been hoping and fantasizing about all day, but Emma was as hot for him as he was for her. She pulled down his boxers, staring up at him with a decadent glance. He braced his hands at the side of his head before his brain exploded as well as the rest of him.

"Emma..." His voice caught, strangled somewhere in his throat.

"I'm right here."

She ran her fingers down the length and leaned forward, warming him with her breath. His body went as rigid as his erection. He sucked in a breath and then released it with a low whoosh.

She glanced up at him with those dark eyes. He'd never forget this sight. She leaned forward and licked the tip. His head instinctively dropped back. Then she glided her tongue down his shaft and back up again. He clenched his jaw as she captured him with a sensual spell. When she took him in her mouth, his knees almost buckled. It felt so good.

Emma added her hand, stroking up and down, as she sucked harder. Shit. He shuddered, captivated by desire that threatened to overwhelm him. He trailed his fingers over her head and moaned. Such incredible sensations.

It was too good. Too much. With reluctance, he pulled her away before he detonated and cut the night short.

"Emma, stop."

"Why?" Her clipped voice was edged with frustration. "I was enjoying that."

"I want to fuck you." Desperation edged his tone.

Her eyes sparkled with lust. "I'm on board with that plan."

He unhooked her bra as he led her to the bed. When she leaned onto it, he pulled her panties down and off. Her naked body was a vision he'd never forget—all that soft skin and luscious curves he yearned to touch. He had to pause as he was already ready to explode. He ran his hand over his mouth and exhaled. He counted to five.

"What's wrong, Vince?" Her brows furrowed.

"Nothing. You're so hot. I just need a moment to regroup." He counted again, making it to three before he couldn't hold off any longer.

He climbed on top of her and kissed her everywhere he could. Her face, her neck, her breasts. He ran his fingers over her silky skin, inhaling the sweet scent of her hair. He touched the delicate skin on her breasts, using his thumb and forefinger to draw her nipples into tight hard peaks that he then licked and sucked while she panted and writhed beneath him.

He'd been desperate to bury himself inside her, but now that he had a taste, he wanted more. He continued kissing down her body, circling her belly button and then shifting lower. The scent of her arousal made him even harder than he'd ever been in his life.

Vince dragged a finger through her slit. He moaned in pleasure. "So wet."

"I want you." Her voice came out breathy and demanding.

He explored her with his fingers as he lowered his head and drank in her scent. When he licked her, she trembled and sighed. So good. He'd never get enough of this. Never wanted to forget it after he left.

After he left…

No, he wouldn't think of that now.

He buried his face between her legs, using both his mouth and hands to draw out her pleasure. Although his cock throbbed, he could play with her this way all night. When he sensed her getting close, he pulled back, driving her closer to the edge each time. The way she responded to his touch with shudders and pleasurable sounds was so satisfying. He wanted to learn a thousand new ways to please her.

Her fingers tangled through his hair. "Vince…" His name was a plea on her lips.

She was bucking off the bed. He had her right there. He couldn't pull back this time, he needed her to come as much as she craved it.

He increased the pressure pushing her the final distance.

She cried out and shattered, clamping tight around his fingers. Her sweet honey covered his tongue, such an addictive taste. He wanted more of it.

"Can't." Her breath came out in audible pants. "Too much." She pulled him up. "Fuck me, Vince."

Hell yes. He moved up over her delicious body, sliding his tip between her folds.

"Condom?"

"Shit." He pulled back. "In my jeans."

VINCE

"I might have some here." She rolled over to her nightstand and fumbled inside the drawer.

A sudden stab of jealousy impaled him.

Why? It shouldn't matter to him who they were for.

But it did.

She pulled out a foil packet. "It might be old. How long do these last?"

He shrugged. "How old do you think it is?"

She glanced at him with a sheepish expression. "Since well before that time with you in the hotel."

Did that mean she hadn't used them since then? He'd been the one to have a condom then. Had she been with another guy since then? He bit the words in, not wanting to picture that.

"You're the only one I've been with since my divorce," she admitted.

He exhaled, relief flooding him in satisfying waves.

But why should he care? They hadn't talked about what last night had meant. For all he knew, it hadn't changed anything for Emma and she still just wanted to be friends with benefits.

He gritted his teeth. That wasn't enough for him. He wanted more.

He wanted her.

Vince shoved that thought aside. It was simply lust talking.

He took the condom packet and read the expiration date. "We're good."

Why was he wasting any more time? He tore open the packet and rolled it down over his shaft. Once sheathed, he crawled back on top of Emma and into her waiting arms.

He kissed her, rubbing the head in between her folds. "Ready for me?"

Her body tensed and then relaxed beneath him. "Yes."

Vince pushed in an inch and then two before she relaxed. With delicious, agonizing slowness he pushed himself deeper until he was fully inside her.

"Ah, sweet fuck." She felt so good. So damn right.

Whatever he's just thought about it just being sex dissipated as one big laughable farce. He wanted Emma now even more than last night. Tomorrow he'd want her even more. It wasn't just sex, wasn't just friendship…

Shut the fuck up.

With his reprimand, he forced himself not to think and just feel. Emma was in his arms again and that's all he needed.

"Yes, Vince."

With slow, gentle movements he moved out and back in. Emma clutched at him. Once they established a rhythm, he lifted her hips off the bed, thrusting deeper. She panted and arched her body against his. He brought his hand down to touch her clit, and she cried out.

"Too sensitive right now." She panted heavily. "From behind?"

He moaned just picturing it. Flipping her onto her hands and knees, he entered her again from this position. He caressed her luscious ass and gave her a quick slap. She yelped and then glanced over her shoulder, her surprised expression turning to desire.

Their pace resumed with him slamming into her from behind. She moaned and pushed her ass back. Their slick, heated bodies meeting again and again with a slapping sound.

He reached forward and stroked Emma. This time she didn't stop him, but melted into his touch, moving with him. He circled her nub and applied more pressure. Her sighs grew louder, moans heightened to soft cries.

"Oh God, Vince, I'm right there!" She trembled and then squeezed around him with hot, tight pulses.

It was too much. Ecstasy thundered through him with uncontrollable force. Vince grabbed her hips as his fiery hot release detonated deep inside her. Quake after quake rushed through him and then subsided.

He lowered his forehead against her shoulder blade.

After several deep, shuddering breaths, he pulled out and removed the condom, tossing it into a trash can. He then lay on his back beside her, rolling her onto him. Her heated naked body pressed against his. Sweet and utter bliss.

Shit.

Sleeping with her was a terrible idea. It just made Vince want her a thousand times more.

If Emma didn't feel the same way about him, where could his feelings lead? Only one outcome—an epic, explosive disaster.

CHAPTER FIFTEEN

EMMA

Emma had a day of errands planned with tidying up her apartment and doing laundry. She also planned to go to a spin class.

After she put her first load of laundry in the dryer, she received a text. She pulled it out of her pocket with a smile, picturing a flirty message from Vince. They'd lingered in bed until late morning when hunger drove them to the kitchen for brunch. At noon, they finally separated and promised to get together that evening.

It wasn't Vince.

Hope you had a good Christmas, Emma.

The text was from her ex, Peter. They rarely communicated after the divorce, so this was odd.

I did. You?

Yes. I know you don't want to hear from me, but I thought it was best that you heard the news from me. We had a surprise.

The next text was a photo of a birth announcement with a festive Christmas theme.

A birth announcement!

Emma stared at it and her skin felt hot. She stared at the proud, excited smile on Peter's face. The exhausted but exhilarated one on his wife. And the tiny, squishy baby nestled in her arms.

Their baby girl was born on Christmas day.

The perfect little Christmas gift for a far-from-perfect man.

Emma's stomach clenched, everything inside her turned taut and churned. She dropped her phone onto the table and started to pace.

He was the one who wronged her. Hurt her. He cheated and got another woman pregnant.

And then what—he gets rewarded for it? What kind of cruel bullshit karma was that?

Her heart quickened and her breath turned ragged.

Not only had he destroyed their marriage, but so much more. Her dreams. Her hopes. Her trust. How could she ever trust someone again when the man she had loved—the one she had thought she'd spend the rest of her life with and start a family with—had started a family with somebody else?

Apparently, she wasn't as special to him as he'd once said. After all, he'd replaced her so fucking easily.

She glanced around the living room, desperate to throw something, break anything!

No, she'd done enough of that when she'd discovered his betrayal. She couldn't let him instigate her like this again.

She had to reply—and not with all the thoughts that churned through her head.

She gritted her teeth and wrote, *Congrats to you all.*

Thanks. You okay?

Need to run. Bye.

Okay, bye.

A few seconds later, he added. *Sorry.*

Again, he was sorry. How many times had he said it? Had he ever truly meant it?

What good was sorry when it didn't take away any of the pain? Sure, it might make him feel better and alleviate some of his guilt.

Did it undo the betrayal?

Nope.

Heal her broken heart?

Nope.

Restore her capacity to trust again?

Absolutely not.

What good was an apology? His words didn't fix anything.

The walls in her apartment were stifling. She had to get out of there. Out of her head.

She had to do something before she let his happiness unravel her. Burn the energy that would eat her from the inside out. Run away from all these suffocating emotions that would drag her back to depths she'd never, ever want to sink to again.

Swim. Yes, that was it. She'd swim.

That was one of the ways she'd dealt with the brutality of her heart being broken. When she swam, she could push herself to a point where she could drown the thoughts, and what she desperately wanted to avoid right now was to think or feel.

Emma changed into her swimsuit and covered up with warmer pants and a hoodie. As she drove to the base, she played her angry woman playlist, one she'd created after discovering Peter's betrayal. Plenty of raw, emotional, heart-pumping songs to choose from, but she skipped right to Alanis Morrissette's *You Oughta Know.*

Once she arrived on base and climbed into the pool, she attempted to soothe her wild, pained thoughts while sluicing through the water. She increased her pace, all too familiar with this chase to disengage from the turbulence in her head.

Her heart pounded faster, and her lungs burned for oxygen.

What was wrong with her for even considering any sort of relationship with Vince? Trust led to heartache. Heartache led to pain. Pain led to the emotional gutting of seeing your ex proudly announcing his new family on Christmas-fucking-day!

Emma swam faster and harder. Her lungs and muscles kicked into hyper drive, almost on the verge of exploding. She almost hoped they would. Then she wouldn't have to feel like this anymore.

She wouldn't have to feel anything.

Half-an-hour later, Emma rinsed the chlorine off in the shower. As the hot water flowed over her body, she took deep breaths, visualizing it washing those negatives thoughts down the drain. She'd tried every sort of yoga and meditation and self-help mantras to help her get through the divorce, and used them now to cope with Peter's announcement.

She'd started a new life without him and was in a better place. No way would she let him continue to drain her emotions like a damn energy vampire.

Maybe she didn't yet know what the future held with her and Vince. That didn't mean she had to let her past with Peter ruin it before she even gave it a chance.

By the time she'd dressed, she'd resolved to not think about Peter and continued on with her day.

That evening, Vince picked up a rotisserie chicken, mashed potatoes, and vegetables and returned to her apartment. When he stepped into her living room, the anguish from Peter's news didn't cut as deep.

As soon as Vince put the food down on the table, she greeted him with passionate kiss.

"What a welcome." He grinned and his eyes gleamed with

delight. "I'll be sure to bring over dinner every night if that's how I'm greeted."

"You don't know how happy I am to see you." She took his hand and led him into her bedroom. "Let's start with dessert."

VINCE

Soon after leaving Emma's the next day, Vince headed to the weight room on base. While he worked on supersets, he thought about Emma. They were growing closer, no doubt. What could that possibly mean for them going forward?

Fuck if he knew. None of his relationships had lasted more than six months, and that longest one had dated back to high school.

He returned to his parents' house and ate a grilled cheese and tomato sandwich with his mother.

"What have you been up to?" his mother asked.

He shrugged. "Staying busy."

"Doing?" she prodded.

"Just came back from working out on base."

"Alone?"

"Yes."

She nodded at him with a knowing look. "Ah ha." Her tone sounded unconvinced.

That's all she was going to get out of him. He didn't want to talk about Emma and face questions he didn't know how to answer.

"What are you doing today?"

"Probably read a bit."

"I'm going to head out to do some errands. Do you need anything?"

"No, thanks, Ma."

After lunch, Vince escaped into his room and pulled out a

fantasy novel to read. After a couple of hours, he checked his messages. Maybe he should send something flirty to Emma.

When he saw an email from Marianne, O'Brien's widow, his muscles tightened. The subject read *Thank You*. A strange tightness clamped his gut, an odd reaction to a thank you.

Considering the context, it made more sense.

He drew a deep breath and then opened the email.

Dear Vince,

Thank you so much for your kindness in sending Christmas presents. The kids loved them all, as you can see in the attached photos.

We're all doing as well as can be expected. I appreciate you asking. It's an adjustment for sure, but we're doing our best.

I hope you are well and that you're enjoying the holidays wherever you are.

Happy new year,
Marianne

Vince opened the first photo. The kids had mile wide smiles as they held up their presents. Emma was right on target with her suggestions. Wrapping paper was scattered about, appearing like a casualty in the battle for gift unveiling.

The next photo was of the entire family in front of the Christmas tree. Nope, not the whole family, just what was left after their unit had been shattered by an IED. Marianne held the youngest and the two other kids stood on either side. They all smiled but Vince could swear he detected a note of sadness underneath, especially in Marianne's expression. The dark circles under her eyes exposed the anguish underneath.

Was she just putting on a brave face for the kids' sake?

Trying to give them some joy this Christmas despite the loss of their father?

Vince's already hardened stomach hollowed out. This wasn't right. O'Brien should have been there.

Despite the brave faces, they'd all be affected by his death—forever. This was their first Christmas without their father or her husband. No amount of money or gifts could lessen that grief. O'Brien was gone. They'd never enjoy a holiday meal as a family again.

That picture ripped through Vince like barbed wire.

He closed the message and shoved the phone into his pocket. He leaned onto his bed and stared at the white circular patterns on the ceiling, the same as he used to do as a teen. Only now his grief eclipsed any of the angst he had when he was younger. He could no longer see the photos, but they were burned onto his memory. He'd tried to do something nice for them but had never felt so useless and hollow.

It should have been him.

It wasn't the first time he had that thought. Countless versions of that idea burned in his brain and no amount of counseling had changed that. Vince didn't have a wife or a family depending on him. It would have been far better for the world for him to have been the one who had been taken out by the IED.

But then he'd pictured his mother's devastation on losing a child. He swallowed a lump. It would destroy her.

Fuck.

He stood and stared out the window, his gaze skimming over one Cape after another. Each house was likely filled with a couple or a family. Or one spouse was home taking care of the family while the other was shipped off overseas. That stress was already high enough. He knew firsthand as his father had been gone for months at a time. Combine that toll with an IED tech sent to deal with explosives and the stakes were even higher.

That was why Marines in his field shouldn't gamble with a family. In an already unsteady game of Jenga, every mission pulled another piece out of the unsteady stack. One wrong move and the entire structure would collapse.

Or explode.

One split second and lives would be destroyed.

If Vince was careless enough to drag someone into his dangerous lifestyle, she could end up like Marianne—a widow forcing a smile on Christmas morning, trying to create some normalcy for her torn-apart family.

Could Vince do that to someone? Someone like Emma?

He swallowed. It was too much of a risk. Too cruel.

And he already cared about her too much.

CHAPTER SIXTEEN

VINCE

Vince attempted to compartmentalize his feelings after reading Marianne's email, but the sharp pain gutted him like a bayonet. He tried to lose himself back in the fantasy novel, but with no luck. Then he sought distraction with video games. Still those photos of O'Brien's family haunted him.

He wanted to be near Emma. Snow was expected tonight, four to six inches. It would have been the perfect night to snuggle inside with Emma, drink hot chocolate and watch a movie or play a game.

When he'd left this morning, he'd said he'd call her later, but he couldn't see her like this—he was too fucked up to be around anyone. With all the shit swarming in his head, any ideas of romance would be smothered by survivor's guilt.

He texted, *Have some family stuff tonight. Stay warm. Maybe we'll get together tomorrow.*

He swallowed. It wasn't technically a lie. He'd be with his family. They'd be doing stuff.

Have a good night, she replied.

He didn't. During dinner, Vince had been even more withdrawn than usual. His parents exchanged glances more than once. Before they selected another puzzle as a weird form of family analysis, he retreated into his room. He put on the *Lord of the Rings* movie in the background and then pulled out his phone. He sought diversion by playing against others in chess, word games, and any sort of trivia to distract him from the chaos in his brain.

And how often he thought of Emma.

The next morning, he moved through the house like a ghost. He responded with minimal conversation with his parents before they went outside to shovel the snow. After they returned inside and warmed up with more coffee, he debated what to do about Emma.

By noon, he gave up trying to stay away.

He texted, *Can I see you later?*

During the two minutes he waited for her reply, muscles corded in his neck. Fuck. He was being selfish by reaching out to her when what he should be doing was creating more distance. He rubbed his muscles to work out the tension.

Sure, she replied.

He exhaled with a low whoosh. *I'm ready when you are.*

I was thinking of cross-country skiing today with all the new snow. Interested?

Sounds great. I don't have equipment, though.

You can rent some there.

When she picked him up that afternoon, her presence comforted him, yet didn't remove the raw hell gnawing at his nerves.

Once they were on the trail head, she asked, "Want to lead?"

"No, it's been years and I'm rusty. I'll follow."

She planted her skis in the established tracks in the snow and started. He followed, awkward in coordinating his limbs until he got into the flow. Once he grew accustomed to the motion, he took in the scenery. With the recent fallen snow, the trees on either side of the path were covered and looked like painted brush strokes. The quiet out here with just the two of them was soothing. They passed a few others as they skied, and the physical exertion didn't leave much time for conversation.

Until he started to think again.

O'Brien's family. The photos. The possible consequence of a relationship with someone in his field.

He fixed his gaze on Emma ahead. She glided so smoothly down the tracks, her dark hair flowing down her back under a red winter hat and her body covered in fitted workout pants and a fleece jacket. He followed along, chasing her. Like chasing a dream.

Was that all this short time with her was? A dream. And then one day he'd wake up to the harsh reality of being deployed once again and facing an IED that could blow him into pieces?

His thoughts twisted down this dark path despite the bright white snow and sun piercing through the pine trees. Shit.

After a couple of hours, they'd both worked up a sweat and were ready for some sustenance. They went home to shower and change and then met up down at one of the wharves at a pub.

He gulped a beer and then ordered another while she was still at the top quarter of her sangria.

"What's going on, Vince? You've been weird all day."

Quiet was nothing new, but the jumpiness was unlike him. He was always the cool one under pressure. He had to be. One jerky motion while he was dismantling an explosive could detonate it. Yet, he was squirming in the booth like someone had slipped leeches down his boxer shorts.

"Nothing, nothing," he lied. "Just thinking."

"About?"

"Some Marine stuff. Nothing you'd want to hear."

"Oh?" She replied. "Why don't you try me?"

He drummed his fingers on the table. "No." He shook his head. "No shop talk while I'm on leave. I have enough of that waiting for me when I go back."

Although he tried to focus on more neutral conversation while he ate a Reuben sandwich, he couldn't shake the image of O'Brien's shattered family from his mind. Was he dragging Emma into a miserable future?

A worry line had formed in between her eyes. Was his anxiety rubbing off on her?

Shit. He rubbed his jaw and squirmed again.

"How's the Caesar wrap?" He forced a neutral tone.

"Fine." She continued to watch him as if trying to read into the chaos inside his skull. "Your Reuben?"

"Great." The upbeat tone sounded as forced as it was. He'd barely taken three bites. His appetite had been squashed like an armored vehicle had trampled the life out of it.

After they left the restaurant, they walked along the water's edge. A few snowflakes fell, the start of another few inches expected tonight.

With recent snowfall blanketing the trees, and the lights twinkling on the water's surface, it was another magical night in Newport during the holidays. But all the joy was sucked out of it.

He shoved his hands into his pocket rather than holding one of hers.

"Vince, seriously, what's going on? It's clear that something is bothering you." Her tone was edged with worry.

He took a deep breath and dropped his head. *Shit. Man up. Speak.*

Otherwise he was prolonging their torment.

Right. He nodded to solidify his resolve.

"You know, you were right all along, Emma."

She glanced "About what?"

"About not dating guys in the military."

She jerked back. He tore his gaze away, avoiding her eyes.

"What do you mean?" she asked.

He fixed his stare on a boat moored farthest from his location. How he wished he could just sail away rather than have this conversation.

Suck it up and do the right thing. It's better for her. Better for you both.

"You're smart to not want to get involved with someone like me." He motioned before him. "You have a new life here in Newport. I'm sent wherever my orders tell me to go."

"Right," she replied in a wary tone. "I've served in the Navy. I know what that's like."

"You said that we could be friends—and maybe now, we're still only friends with benefits. But it can't work that way."

"What? Why not?"

Because I care about you. Because I want more than that from you.

He pulled the metaphorical pin.

"Because our relationship has developed into something more intense, at least for me. That can't be good for either of us."

She blinked a couple of times and rubbed between her brows but didn't say anything.

"You deserve better." He grimaced before he uttered the words. "I can't do this anymore."

And tossed the metaphorical grenade.

Why did it feel like he was blowing up his own chance at happiness as well as hers?

"What the?" Her mouth widened into an O. "What is this?"

"Emma, I'm uh—" Fuck, this was worse than he thought it would be. "Please don't make this any harder than it needs to be," he pleaded.

"Harder than it needs to be?" she echoed with a tone between surprise and sarcasm.

"Right."

"Vince."

"What?"

"Look at me," she demanded.

He brought his gaze back to her. The surprised expression was gone, replaced by fury. Pure, clear anger.

"If you're going to pull this shit, you can at least have the decency to look me in the eye."

He swallowed. This sucked. He knew this wasn't going to be easy, but... fuck!

"I don't know who the hell you think you are trying to play me like this." She raised her index finger and pointed at his chest.

"Emma, I'm not trying to hurt—"

"I'm not done." She stepped closer. "You're playing games with me. *I don't do games. I don't do drama.*"

"I'm not playing games with you." He raised both hands palms up. "I'm trying to do the right thing here."

"Ha! The right thing? You're portraying yourself as the good guy here?"

"I'm trying to keep you from getting hurt."

"Don't patronize me, Vince." She pointed at him. "You're trying to protect yourself."

His eyes widened. Her words hit him like a fresh slap. "What?"

"I should have known better. No, I did. But I fooled myself by thinking you were different. But you're just. Like. Them." She poked him hard in the chest.

Anger roiled through him. "What the fuck, Emma? You're the one who ran out on me. Then you didn't want me. And then you only want me as a fuck buddy. You never indicated you wanted me for anything more than sex while I'm in town, so who's the one playing games here?"

"Fuck buddy?" Her pitch rose. "Oh, you're such a fucking saint!" Her expression contorted with fury.

He raised his hands to his temples. "Damn it, Emma. I care about you. Can't you see that?"

She scowled. "Not at all."

He took a deep breath, trying to sort through their train wreck. "I'm everything you don't want. You told me that from the beginning and I get it. I can't give you anything. No security. No promise that I'd be there for your birthday or Christmas. Nothing."

She raised both hands before dropping them with a frustrating slap to her sides. "Don't give me bullshit excuses. I've heard so many over the years, I can give your goddamn speech for you." She shook her head. "First with my father."

Where was this mention of her father from out of nowhere? She'd never mentioned him before. "What?"

"Then, there was that hell with Peter. And now..." She gave a mirthless laugh and hateful look. "You're so damn righteous!"

Pedestrians across the street glanced over. A growl rumbled in his chest.

"Please," he pleaded in a lower tone. "Can we talk this out?"

"No." She raised one hand, palm out. "I'm too screwed up. I warned you I had issues."

"We're all screwed up in some way."

She blinked a few times. "Yeah, maybe. She snorted. "Well, here's the rundown of my pathetic family life and shitty choices since. My father was in the Army. He'd go away for trainings and things. We discovered those were lies. He had another woman and a kid in another state. *Another family!* He lived a double life for two years, and we didn't have a clue. Apparently, we weren't good enough for him."

Vince's heart ached for her. "That's awful. I'm so sorry." His family might drive him crazy, especially with the way they poked into his privacy, but he appreciated that they were close.

He had no doubt they loved him, and he loved them too. He took a step toward Emma.

She stepped back. "That's not the end of it, though." She released a mirthless laugh. "I married a guy who cheated on me. He got another woman pregnant, someone who was also married. Two more marriages destroyed. And then they lost the baby. So much pain for everyone involved." She blew out a rough breath. "But she got pregnant again and they got married. He texted me yesterday to let me know they had their baby on Christmas morning." She scowled. "How sweet. He gets a reward for being a shitty husband who violated all our vows." Her tone was rough with bitterness. "And me? What do I get?" She pointed between them. "This." Her eyes blazed with shiny tears. "I fall for a guy who doesn't want me. What a fuckin' idiot I am to think this would be different." She shook her head. "I've had enough."

She'd fallen for him too? With the way she glared at him with both fiery anger and gut-wrenching anguish, it was hard to believe. But he did want her—so fuckin' much it hurt.

His resolve melted. All he wanted to do was sweep away every stupid thing he'd said tonight and just take her in his arms, hold her and kiss her and not let her go until he had to.

"Emma," he began, not sure where to even go from there.

She released a shaky exhale and raised her hand, palm facing him. "Enough."

Her sharp tone snapped some sense into him. The last thing he wanted to do was hurt her.

Emma sucked in a jerky breath, turned, and strode down the dock. Vince stepped toward her, her name on his lips to call her. The overwhelming urge to run to her and take it all back made his feet itch. He clenched his fists and forced himself to stop.

It was better that he let her go.

He stared at her retreating figure fighting the compulsion to follow until she disappeared into the darkness. And still, the longing remained.

EMMA

How had Emma let this happen?

She broke into a power walk to get away from Vince before she crumbled. Her jaw clenched, muscles pounded with rage, and veins pumped with fury. Her heart was shredding, but no way would she let him see her cry.

Only once she was certain that he was out of view did she turn and face the harbor. She let the hot tears rain down.

Oh, she was such a damn fool! She should have listened to the voice in the beginning that warned her not to get involved with Vince. How had she managed to put on rose-colored glasses when gazing at Vince, distorting the ugliness of reality? Relationships like this didn't work. They crashed and crushed.

For several minutes, she let the tears flow, swimming in an ocean of remorse. The snow had picked up while she stewed in the shit storm that was her life.

Wait, she couldn't keep beating herself up over things she couldn't change. What she could change was her reaction to them. She took deep breaths to calm her racing heartbeat and stared at the falling snowflakes. She'd get through this.

If the saying of what didn't kill you made you stronger had any validity, she was Xena the Warrior Princess by now.

CHAPTER SEVENTEEN

VINCE

Vince took the beer from Angelo and took a swig from the bottle. The icy coldness rolled over his tongue. "Hits the spot."

"Gotta get them while you can," Angelo said.

"True." Having a Narragansett Lager beer while deployed would be as elusive as spotting a yeti.

Angelo sat at the other end of the sofa in his living room. Vince had borrowed his father's car to visit, needing an excuse to get away from Newport. He was too close to Emma there and the feelings after that epic disaster were still too raw.

Angelo flipped through the options on Netflix.

"Right there," Vince noted when he spotted *Arrested Development.*

"Ah, yes. Matty still greets me with 'Hey brother,'" Angelo said in the way Buster referred to his brothers in the show.

Vince snorted in acknowledgment. "Same here. Too bad he couldn't make it this Christmas."

"Right. Don't make me miss the pain in the ass." Angelo grinned.

"Unfortunately, he's probably going to have a shitty New Year's Eve as well."

"Not Matty. He'll find a way to make the best of it." Angelo took a sip of his beer.

"True," Vince agreed. Matty always had a mischievous smile to go with the joke on his lips.

Angelo raised his chin to Vince. "What are your plans? Going out with Emma?"

Vince flinched on hearing her name. He attempted to cover it up by taking a gulp of beer. A long gulp.

"Ah, I knew something was up," Angelo added. "Ma has been pestering me to find out. She said you were even quieter and more reclusive than usual last night and this morning. And that's saying something when it comes to you."

A bitter aftertaste coated Vince's tongue, which had nothing to do with the beer. After he had left Emma yesterday, he'd walked and walked until the cold night air drove him home. Still, his mind looped in circles with questions over what the fuck had just happened, so he isolated himself in his room. He thought about what she'd said about her father and what she'd just learned from her ex. Since he was fucked up himself after seeing the pictures of O'Brien's family, his timing to try to talk to her couldn't have been worse. All their raw emotions collided in a perfect storm of past wounds and current baggage that spiraled like an uncontrollable force in a turbulent sky.

Vince groaned and exhaled through clenched teeth. "It's over."

Angelo stared at him. "What happened?"

Vince rose. He couldn't sit there on Angelo's couch while he eyed him in that elder brother way, assessing whether Vince had fucked up.

Because that was the rock-solid truth.

Vince paced across the living room and paused in front of a bookshelf. The top two shelves were filled with medical and science books, but on the lower shelves were plenty of mysteries, thrillers, and even a few romances. His eyes fixed on a wedding picture from Angelo and Catherine's wedding. His parents stood on either side of the bride and groom and then he and Matty stood by like bookends in their matching penguin suits. Back when Angelo said he was getting married, Vince thought he was nuts, but marriage and civilian life seemed to suit Angelo. He was happy.

But that was the critical difference—Angelo was a civilian now. Vince had no intentions of leaving the Marines.

"We were having a good time while I was on leave, that was all."

Angelo hmphed. "Don't bullshit me. I know that tone."

Vince groaned. That was the problem with talking to Angelo, someone who could read him far too well. "Fine." Vince huffed. "I blew it."

"How?"

Vince's one-shoulder shrug was taut with tension. "I'd sent O'Brien's family Christmas gifts. His wife sent me an email to thank me. When I saw the picture of them—the family with their first Christmas without O'Brien. I don't know—it hit me right here." He tapped his chest.

Angelo's expression tightened to a near wince. "Shit. That's rough."

Vince rubbed his temples. "After that, all this shit started to unravel in my head. What Emma and I were doing. Whether we could even have a future." He scowled. "When I tried talking about it, I didn't do it well. My thoughts fell out as chaotic as what was in my brain, and I pushed her away. It went FUBAR fast. Like grenade launcher fast with a similar outcome—fuckin' disastrous explosion."

Angelo grunted. "In other words, you were chicken-shit and retreated to somewhere you thought was safer."

Vince grunted. His brother didn't mince his words and in a strange way it was what he needed to hear. "Maybe."

Angelo leaned forward. "Listen, I get it. We've all lost people and it sucks. It fuckin' rips you up inside. I've been there. It will continue to do so if you let it."

"What do you do?" Vince noted pain etched on Angelo's face. Before he'd left the SEALs, Angelo had admitted that seeing his buddy die and being unable to save him had messed him up. It had made him reevaluate his life and had contributed to his decision to leave the Navy, starting a new life with Catherine in Providence.

"It's not easy. Survivor's guilt might always be a part of you, like a shadow. Brooding doesn't change what happened or bring them back. You have to find the reasons that keep you going—just like O'Brien's family is doing. They're doing their best to continue their lives. This might be the worst Christmas ever, but they're still carrying on. That's what O'Brien would have wanted for them." Angelo leaned back and fixed his gaze on Vince. "And for you."

Vince rubbed his jaw. "Knowing doesn't make it any easier to accept." He peeled a corner of the label from the bottle. "I just want to numb myself and not think. Maybe drink until I find peace with oblivion."

"Nope." Angelo gave a resolute nod. "That never happens. It just makes things a thousand times worse."

Vince threw a hand up. "Well, what do you suggest?"

Angelo glanced around. "Let's get you out of here and get you some fresh air to start." He stood. "I have tomorrow off. How about we go to the mountains? Get some skiing in?"

That had been something their entire family would do during winter breaks growing up. "It's been a long time since

I've gone downhill skiing. I don't know if I'll even remember how."

"You will. I picked it up again once I moved here. Just take a lesson in the morning to get the right form and you'll be good to go."

Vince stared at Angelo. It wasn't a bad idea. Maybe it would give him a break from the looping thoughts in his head. "Yeah, all right."

EMMA

After a fitful night of sleep, Emma woke to her phone ringing. It was Karine.

"Hello?" Emma's voice croaked.

"You okay?"

"Yeah." She rubbed her hand through her hair. "No."

"What happened?"

Emma sighed. "You have a minute?" She added, "A long minute."

AN HOUR LATER, EMMA ENTERED KARINE'S SHOP. THE CHIMES ON the door announced her arrival. The scent of soup and baked goods wrapped around her. Her stomach growled in response, yet she still had no appetite.

Karine came out of the back room, her white apron smeared with colors like a Picasso painting. She had a dusting of flour across her jawline.

Emma forced a smile. "Looks like you're getting ready for an art show." She pointed at Karine's apron.

Karine waved her hand in a dismissive motion. "I had a little snafu back there." She leaned her head back and sighed. "Thanks for helping out today and tomorrow. I know not most people want to work on New Year's Eve. One of my girls called in 'sick.'" Karine punctuated the doubts of her employee's illness with air quotes. "She'll probably have this 'illness' until the new year starts."

Emma shrugged. "Sure, why not? I'm happy to help. It's not like I have any plans tomorrow night."

"Might as well make some money." Karine rubbed her fingers together. "It would've been nice to celebrate our first New Year's together as a family, but I couldn't turn down this gig. New Year's Eve prices are some of my best."

"And it's not like Laura will know one date from the next. She won't be missing anything. You'll be spending time with her on New Year's Day."

"That's the plan. Although mama guilt finds a way to sneak up on me no matter what."

"It shouldn't. You're a great mom. And look, you're running your own successful business. One day Laura will grow up and look up to you—and appreciate all you've done for her."

"Thanks." Karine grinned. "I'm guessing it's not going to be during the teenage years."

"Oh no." Emma spread her hands to the side. "That's when you'll be her worst enemy."

They laughed and went back into the kitchen area. Karine pointed to one of the massive soup pots. "Feel free to have a bite before you get started. Maybe a cup of Italian wedding soup?"

Italian wedding. Emma grimaced. Those two words reminded her of the summer when she'd met a hot Italian Marine at a wedding. Since she'd walked into the shop, Emma had been grateful for Karine avoiding the elephant-in-the-room talk with the aftermath of what had happened with Vince. When Karine had called to see if Emma wanted to pick up the New Year's gig, she had given her the condensed version from Peter's text all the way through her storming away from Vince.

And then she remembered Vince use a similar mention—

he'd joked about an elephant in the backseat when she was driving him to the high school.

Damn, hopefully soon she'd get to a time without things reminding her of him.

Emma forced a smile. "Smells great, but I'm not that hungry."

"When's the last time you ate?" Karine asked with a worried mom expression.

Emma shrugged. "I'll eat after we get some stuff done. What can I do to start?"

Karine pointed out dozens of cupcakes in various states of frosting and nakedness. "You can frost the rest of the cupcakes." She offered Emma pink frosted one. "A little sugar to get you going."

Emma stared at the cupcake and recoiled. She tried to cover it up with a shake of her head. Sure, Karine was trying to take care of her and cheer her up, but the cupcake was yet another reminder. The whole flirtation over the fallen cupcakes at Vince's brother's wedding.

"Emma?"

"What?"

"I offered you a cupcake, and you looked like I handed you a knife for self-sacrifice."

Emma shook her head. "Sorry. I'm happy to frost them. I'm just—bleh. You know?"

"I know," Karine replied. "You'll get over this."

Emma gave a dismissive wave. "It's for the better."

"Maybe," Karine conceded. "But you might be looking at things too black and white when it's really various shades of gray."

"What do you mean?"

Karine picked up a spoon and stirred the contents of her mixing bowl with vigor. "You never really gave this a chance. You swore off any man in the military as if they're all the same.

But that's not true. Are you the same as all the women you served with?"

"No, but..." Emma straightened. Karine had some truth in that insight. "Still, you know what they say about fool me once, and fool me twice. Well, if I allow myself to be fooled three damn times, then I deserve all the misery I get."

Karine scoffed at that with a doubtful sound. "Don't let some old saying affect you. That's all it is—words."

Emma exhaled with a whoosh. "If I don't learn from experience, then I'm a sucker asking for more misery."

Karine tilted her head and gave Emma a sage look. "All right, I can see why you'd go there. Not that I necessarily agree with it."

"Why not?"

"If you go into a relationship expecting to be hurt, you're bound to find a reason to prove that."

Emma adjusted her stance. There could be a kernel of truth in Karine's words.

"It sounds like you're using your past as a crutch to keep you from finding happiness in your future." Karine arched her brows. "And the present."

CHAPTER EIGHTEEN

VINCE

Vince stared at the scenery as he ascended on the chairlift with Angelo. On the initial rides up the chairlift, they'd tried to identify wildlife tracks or types of trees. As the day went on, their conversations had turned deeper. They'd touched on life, family, the military, goals. That was one of the things Vince remembered about days on the mountains. The cool mountain air and vast blue sky without any obstructions from buildings provided some clarity. Maybe some distance would give him a bit more perspective about Emma.

"I've been trying to let this thing with Emma go, so I can go on with my life," he admitted on their final ride before the lifts shut down.

"But—" Angelo prodded. "I hear the doubts in your voice."

"Exactly." Vince swung his skies a few inches in each direction. "I don't know if that's what I want anymore." He glanced at Angelo. "Look at you. You walked away from everything and started over. How did you know that's what you wanted?"

"I had my reasons. I felt the toll and knew it would start to affect my work. I wouldn't be helping anyone if I couldn't do my job properly. It was time to leave."

Angelo faced ahead, and it was difficult for Vince to read his expression with the helmet and goggles, but he could hear Angelo's introspective tone.

"Any regrets about leaving the SEALs?"

"None. I lucked out to be with an amazing woman who I'm building a new life with." After a few seconds, Angelo added, "But, that was me. We might be brothers, but we're different. Always have been. Different dreams, different goals. It doesn't matter what I've done. You need to figure out what you want."

Vince stared at the mountain peak ahead. The late afternoon had dipped lower in the bluebird sky in the distance.

"That's the problem. Once I was so sure about everything. I'd serve my twenty years—single—and then when I was ready to retire from the Marines, that's when I'd finally think about settling down. I mean I'd still be fairly young then—late thirties."

"And now?"

"There are doubts."

"Like what?"

"That keeping everyone at arm's length and putting one part of my life on hold isn't the right way after all."

"Everyone?" Angelo's voice lifted in question.

"Okay, one person in particular."

"Hmm…"

"Fine, Emma," Vince added.

"Now we're getting somewhere. The way I'm seeing it as an outsider is that you were both happy together. By trying to keep yourselves from being hurt, you've made yourselves miserable."

Vince exhaled. There might be a bit of insight in his older brother's words. Vince smirked. "Now you're sounding like a shrink."

"Then you shouldn't be surprised by what I'm going to ask you next." Angelo turned to Vince. "What are you going to do?"

Vince stared again at the peak above as if it might provide some insight. With that clear sky and clean mountain air, surely he'd find the missing piece that would solve his puzzle.

What stretched beyond that mountain remained a mystery.

"Good question." Vince nodded to himself. "I'm still trying to figure it out."

"By thinking?" Angelo asked.

That was the usual way Vince would go. He'd retreat into himself and think and think. Would that give him any insight into what Emma wanted, though?

No. By doing.

"I should start by talking to Emma."

When Vince arrived back in Newport on the afternoon of December 31st, he called Emma. She didn't answer, so he left a message asking if they could talk.

A few hours passed, and she hadn't returned his call.

He went into the kitchen to get a glass of water and then sat in the living room with his parents.

"Are you going out tonight?" his mother asked.

"No plans yet." Would that change when Emma called him back?

If she called him back.

"Come out with us."

"What are you doing?"

"Our usual," his father replied. "We go out to dinner and come back here."

"We watch the celebrations on TV," his mother added. "You know neither one of us will stay awake until midnight, though."

Was that what couples did after many years together—had their traditions? It didn't sound as exciting as going out to count down the seconds until midnight. But then again, being alone with your loved ones was better than being in a crowd full of strangers.

"Sure, I'll come out to dinner." But hopefully he wouldn't ring in the new year alone on his parents' couch.

They went out to an Italian restaurant downtown and were home by eight. Vince checked his phone for what was probably the thirtieth time since he'd called her. No missed calls or voicemails.

Damn. He texted her: *Just making sure you got my message. Can we talk?*

He killed the next hour playing chess on his phone while waiting for a reply.

Shit. How could he reach her?

"Can I borrow your car?" he asked his mother.

"To go where?"

"See a friend."

She stared at him with a knowing mom look. "You need to be careful." She raised her index finger. "Too many drunk drivers. Just get where you need to go and stay put."

"Will do." He gave her a hug. "Happy New Year."

He drove to Emma's apartment. He rang the bell a few times before he gave up. She either wasn't home or didn't want to see him.

Now what?

He wasn't ready to give up yet.

One person might be able to help him. But the odds of her being around on New Year's Eve were slim. After he looked up the catering shop where Emma had mentioned helping out her friend, he drove downtown.

The lights were on. Someone was inside.

He pulled open the glass door.

The dark-haired woman rolling dough on a massive stainless-steel counter glanced up. "Can I help you?"

"Are you Karine?"

"Yes."

"I'm Vince. A friend of Emma's."

"Oh." She gave him a long look appraising him. "And you're looking for her here? Tonight?"

Vince squared his jaw and then rolled his neck. "I need to talk to her."

Karine sprinkled some flour on her rolling pin. "A phone would work." She returned to her rolling.

He exhaled with a slow breath. She wasn't going to make it easy. "She hasn't returned my call or text."

Karine flipped the dough. "She's busy. Or she doesn't want to talk to you."

Vince resisted groaning. "We need to talk. The last time…" He shook his head. "I need to tell her how I feel."

Karine stopped rolling and stared at him. "Don't hurt her."

Vince ran his hand over his hair and pressed his lips together tight. "I would never. I care about her too much. Will you please help me reach her?"

Karine shook her head. "I'm too busy tonight. We both are. The hotel gave us a misprint with the number of guests and I'm scrambling to adjust."

His ears perked. "We?" He glanced around the shop, searching for a peek of Emma behind one of the massive freezers.

When his gaze returned to Karine, her mouth spread with a knowing grin. "Wait. I just thought of something."

"What?"

"We help each other out."

"How?"

"Do you have a car?"

"Yes."

"Great, I'm swamped here. I'm so grateful Emma could help out."

"Emma's here?" His eyes took another spin around the catering shop.

"No, she's at the hotel. If you want to see her, it's going to cost you." She raised one brow and grinned.

Always a price to pay, wasn't there? "What is it?"

"If you can take this batch up to Providence, you can see Emma." She motioned around her. "It'll make it easier for me to finish up the desserts."

Vince's lips widened. He liked the sass on this one. "You've got yourself a deal." He stepped over to the table with stacked pans. "Just tell me where to take them."

She shook her head and muttered. "Emma's going to kill me for this, but I think it's the best plan. You two need to talk." She arched her brows. "Or kill each other. Whatever." She gestured with a wave. "That's as far as I'm going to get involved." She clapped her hands. "All right, move it, Marine. We're already behind schedule." She pointed at a stack of covered pans. "Get those to the hotel pronto."

He grinned at Karine as she snapped into the directness of the drill instructor. "On it, ma'am."

THE SCENT OF THE BAKED GOODS WAS TOO TEMPTING DURING THE drive to Providence. Although Vince had already eaten at the restaurant earlier and his stomach was tight with knots over what he was about to do, he couldn't resist sneaking a cupcake from beneath the covered pan next to him. As he took a bite of the sweet frosting and chocolate cake, he practically heard Karine scold him for messing with the arrangement.

A hotel tower appeared on the right. He pulled up in the loading area and then carried the trays into the kitchen, abuzz with the frenzy of scents of the event.

He approached the closest person, a man wearing an apron, and said, "These are from Karine's Catering."

"Great. We're running low." The man directed him to a table.

After Vince completed that task, he searched for Emma amid the chaotic thrum of the hotel staff in the kitchen. The muscles at the back of his neck corded. Would he find her? If so, how would she react?

No sign of Emma with the kitchen staff.

He entered a ballroom and the sound of soft jazz filled his ears. It was already boisterous with New Year's Eve festivities. Ornate chandeliers hung overhead. Black and silver party decorations covered from walls to tables to chairs. Couples in their finest suits and dresses danced while others sat at the tables and ate or drank. In black pants and a royal blue button-down shirt, he wasn't dressed for the event, but he wasn't here to join them.

There she was.

His heart thudded like rapid-fire ammo.

Adjusting dessert plates at one of the buffet tables, she wore black slacks and a white blouse, just like she had at Angelo's wedding. Her hair was pulled back into some type of twisty bun.

As he walked over to her, his tongue seemed to thicken in his mouth. His hands turned clammy. He wiped them along the sides of his pants.

He forced himself to slow his breaths as he approached. "Hello, Emma."

She turned so quickly, she bumped the table. Plates jangled in protest. "Vince." She took in a sharp breath. "What are you doing here?"

"Careful." He grinned. "We wouldn't want a cupcake catastrophe."

CHAPTER NINETEEN

EMMA

Emma's mouth dropped open as she stared at Vince. "What? How did you know I'd be here?"

"Karine sent me on a mission—with a price."

Emma blinked and shook her head. "I don't understand. What's going on?"

"I've been trying to reach you, so we can talk. When you didn't respond, I went down to Karine's shop to see if she'd help me find you. She agreed—on the condition that I'd deliver more desserts."

Emma's lips twitched, and she wasn't sure if she wanted to curse or smile. That sounded like Karine—playing matchmaker while also being practical about business. "You two conspired over cupcakes?"

Vince responded with a sheepish expression. "Perhaps. To fulfill my end of the bargain, I need to let you know that more desserts are in the kitchen."

She glanced around the ballroom and wiped her hands on the apron. "Vince, I'm working. This is a bad time."

Not that she could think of a good time. Yes, she'd listened to his voice mail earlier and read his text. She wasn't ready to talk to him yet and needed some space before she responded. The emotional upheaval from their last conversation was too much.

But, seeing him here at the hotel in Providence hit her with another blast of emotion, not all of which she could decipher. She didn't know how to deal with it. She sighed, her mind going haywire. "Where are the desserts?"

"Come with me." He led them into the kitchen and pointed at stacked pans. "Voila."

At least they were out of the ballroom, away from inquisitive eyes. This discussion wasn't one she wanted to have with any witnesses. She had to act professionally as she was representing Karine and her business.

When a staff member opened the door leading back to the ballroom, the music turned louder. The door closed, muffling the sound. She needed to get back out there. "We can't talk now."

"Understood. When are you finished working?"

"Well after midnight. The party ends at one and we need to clean up."

"I can help. Or I can wait for you in the lobby."

He sounded so sincere and eager to be with her.

She met his gaze and sighed. "Vince…"

"What?"

She raised a hand near her temple and then lowered it, shuffling her feet. "You're leaving soon. Why even have this conversation?"

"That's the thing." He stepped closer to her. "I don't want to leave without us talking about it. Look, I know I upset you and I'm sorry. I freaked out too and have a thousand regrets."

Curious to hear more, she didn't know what to say. So many questions formed on her lips, but she had to get the desserts out to replenish what was rapidly disappearing from the tables. "Come with me. We can talk while we work."

She directed him on how to display the cupcakes and restock the desserts in a tasteful presentation. Once they'd finished, she retreated near the wall behind the tables to keep an eye on things.

Vince stood beside her.

"I still don't understand why you're here."

Vince closed his eyes and exhaled. "I know you're busy, so I'll make it quick. Remember how you helped me shop for O'Brien's kids?"

"Yes."

"His wife emailed to thank me and sent photos. The family photo without him in it—knowing he never would be…" Vince took a deep breath and exhaled. "It hit me in a bad way. I'm not using it as an excuse, but that's why I was acting so weird."

Her heart ached for him. "I wish you'd told me."

"I wish I had, too." He gave her a lopsided grin. "You once said you had more issues than the periodical section. Guess you're not the only one. We all have hang-ups, right?"

She parted her lips, not sure what to say.

Vince squared his jaw and continued. "Instead of talking to you, I retreated. I'm sorry. The thing is I care about you and I never want to hurt you. I've told myself I don't want to be in a relationship with someone while I'm a Marine because it's too difficult. The consequences like what happened with O'Brien's family are devastating. But maybe I'm just being too much of a chicken shit to put myself out there." He reached for her hand as they stood side-by-side back against the wall. "The thing is, Emma, I've fallen for you. Hard. And I hope you'll give me a chance to prove myself worthy of you." He squeezed her hand. "I'm not your ex. I'm not your father." After a pause, he added,

"I'm just a man who's falling in love, and I want to make you happy."

Emma's heartbeat quickened. His words swam through her brain filling her with happiness. Yet the reminders of Peter and her father sliced her, reminding her of the potential for pain.

Why couldn't she just take the leap and see? What was the worst that could happen?

They'd crash.

She pulled her hand away. "I can't." She turned to face him and stepped back.

All the hopeful expectation drifted from his eyes. "Why?"

Her breath came quicker. "I'm afraid."

"I'm afraid too. But not as much as living a life with you not in it."

She shook her head. "I can't be hurt again. I'm not strong enough."

His chest rose and fell as he searched her eyes. "You are the strongest, most caring woman I know. I'd never hurt you, Emma. I swear it."

"You can't promise that."

He took a deep breath and exhaled. "You're right. That's what worries me too." He squeezed his eyes shut and then reopened them. "I could never prevent what happened to O'Brien's family and the pain they're going through."

She covered her heart. So many overwhelming emotions. She needed time to process them—and process all that Vince had said. But not now. Not if she wanted to make it through this shift without crumbling in the corner of the kitchen. A lump formed in her throat. In a strangled voice she managed to say, "Please go."

His mouth opened with a surprised look. In the next blink, an impassive one was snapped into place. His mask. She'd was likely wearing her own right now.

He bristled and then rolled his shoulders back. "I understand. I shouldn't have bothered you." He rubbed the back of his neck. "I hope your new year is your happiest yet. You deserve the best." He turned and walked away.

She watched him leave and gulped. Stepping forward, she raised her hand to call him back.

A middle-aged woman stumbled along the table and when she reached for a cupcake, she tipped her champagne glass and spilled some over the tablecloth. She stumbled away with her dessert, oblivious to the mess she'd made.

Shit. Emma rushed over with a rag. As she blotted the liquid from the white tablecloth, she turned back and spotted the blue of Vince's shirt just before he retreated into the sea of black and white.

She exhaled and a lump felt like it moved from her throat to settle into her gut. It was better for him to walk away. That way no one risked any more pain. It could only lead to a mess like the one she had to clean up, but with much more emotional turmoil.

VINCE

What a damn fool he was.

Vince walked through the crowd of couples dancing in their finest black-tie suits and evening gowns. Was he out of his mind? Did he really think Emma would leap into his arms, ready to ride off into the sunset with him like this was some happy ending to a movie?

No, of course not. This was the real world and people got hurt. Hearts were broken and lives were torn apart. Why had he put on blinders and attempted to live out some sort of fantasy?

Angelo. He groaned. Just because Angelo had found a way to play house, didn't mean that Vince could—and definitely not while he was an EOD tech. Long ago he'd made his peace with his choice of career. Sure, that might mean a lonely future, but that was the path he had chosen to take.

Where the hell should he go now? Back to Newport? Back to his parents' house where they were probably already asleep?

Since Angelo lived nearby, Vince stepped into the lobby, pulled out his phone, and texted him.

Hey man, I'm here in Providence.

What are you doing here? Angelo replied.

Feeling like an ass.

Why?

Emma's here working at a hotel. I tried to talk to her. It didn't work out.

Shit, man. Sorry about that. Hey, but at least you know. It's better than wondering.

I suppose.

Want to come over?

Vince pictured it. He'd interrupt Angelo and Catherine's quiet—and probably romantic situation. *No, I'll just head back home.*

You sure? It's low key. We're just hanging out. Have some champagne for the toast and some snacks.

Why had he even texted Angelo? Just to vent? *I'm not going to ruin your night with my misery.*

Want me to come down there? We can get a drink.

No, man. I'll just walk around here before I head back to Newport. Happy new year.

Happy new year.

THE BRIGHT EYES AND LAUGHTER THAT SURROUNDED VINCE MADE him bristle. He had to get away from all these people celebrating.

What a way to start the new year. The only certainty in his

future was that it was out of his control. He'd be sent where he was needed.

And apparently on his own.

Well shit, he was a Marine. If there was one thing he'd learned in the Corps, it was to adapt and overcome.

His phone buzzed. It was Angelo.

Don't leave. We're coming to you.

Vince's lips twitched into a grin. Angelo couldn't help but be the caretaker. That had been his role since they were kids. Maybe Vince shouldn't have texted him, but he was glad his brother and sister-in-law were on the way.

Spending New Year's Eve with family was better than spending it rejected and alone.

CHAPTER TWENTY

EMMA

*E*mma forced herself to focus on replenishing cupcakes and desserts instead of the thousand questions buzzing in her head.

Karine arrived and glanced around the ballroom. "Well?"

"Well what?"

"Did Vince come?"

Emma clucked her tongue. "Yes. I put the desserts out already. I think we're in good shape now."

Karine planted her hands on her hips. "What happened with him?"

"Nothing." Emma glanced at the celebration. Was Vince still out there? No, why would he be? He was likely halfway back to Newport by now. She motioned at the tables. "We have enough going on tonight."

Karine raised a brow. "Let me worry about that. You didn't talk to him?"

Emma pinned her gaze on Karine. "A little. Thanks for the heads up, by the way. Talk about blindsiding me."

Karine shooed that with a wave. "Blindsided, how? The poor man wanted to talk to you. What's wrong with that?"

Emma sighed. "You know exactly what's going on."

Karine's expression turned nonchalant. "So, maybe you two can get a room here tonight and—*talk*."

Emma groaned. "Not happening. I asked him to leave."

"You what?" Karine's eyes widened.

"It's not that simple, Karine, and you know it." Emma bit her lip. "We have too many complications to make anything work."

"Oh, you can't fool me with that excuse." Karine waved again. "That's just you trying to protect yourself. But I've seen how happy you were with him. And tonight, I saw a guy who is so crazy about you, that he came to see me and brought desserts up here to Providence just to have the chance to talk to you." She raised her index finger. "If you can't see that, then we need to take you to an optometrist right away."

After Karine called her out, Emma threw her hands up. "What does it matter? He's leaving soon. *Leaving*. I know how the military works and dealing with separations is tough. We're better off going our own ways. That way nobody gets hurt."

"And nobody feels anything. They merely exist." Karine's words hung in the air like a rain cloud, adding to Emma's sense that she might have made a mistake.

All she wanted to do was wrap herself in a bubble, that way no one got hurt. "You don't know what it's like, Karine. John adores you. He'd never hurt you."

"Life is full of pain, Emma. Love sometimes more. But with the right person, it's all worth it."

Emma shuffled her feet. Was there any truth to that?

"If you can't take a chance on chasing happiness, you'll never find it." Karine clapped her hands. "And on that note, I'm back to work. You're a grown woman and you can make your own decisions."

After she walked away, Emma's doubts rose to the bright, sparkling chandeliers. Had she made a mistake by pushing Vince away tonight?

She stared at the clock. The minutes counted down to that significant midnight hour—to a new year she might start with regret.

VINCE

Vince paced through the hotel lobby. A pop made him duck. Shit, it was only one of those mini champagne poppers. Not a treat for anyone who dealt with explosives for a living. He attempted to slow his breathing.

Angelo and Catherine arrived less than fifteen minutes later.

Angelo noted, "We lucked out with a Lyft."

"Thanks for coming." Vince greeted them both. He turned to Catherine. "I'm sorry I dragged you out too."

Catherine waved her hand. "We're family now, Vince." She grinned. "I'm glad we came. Otherwise, we'd be settling into the role of old married couple far too quickly."

Angelo scanned the lobby. People milled about drifting from the ballroom. "Come on, let's find someplace to go besides this stuffy hotel."

Twenty minutes later, Vince, Angelo and Catherine squeezed into a sports bar around the corner from the hotel.

Once they had their drinks and a spot at a high-top, Vince raised his glass. "Happy New Year." His tone lacked any enthusiasm.

Angelo noted, "It could be worse, right?"

Vince grunted. "True. I've had some rough ones."

Catherine asked, "Do you want to talk about what happened?"

"Nope." Vince took a big sip of his beer and stared at the glass. "I'm guessing my big brother told you."

"He gave me the gist of it." Her voice was gentle.

Vince shook his head. "How did I fuck this up so badly?"

"You didn't." Angelo patted him on the back. "You gave it a shot and that's all you can do. She made her decision for whatever reasons she had. It sucks, but you move on."

"She thinks of me no better than her father and her ex-husband, both who were in the military and cheated on their wives. She thinks I'll do the same."

Catherine nodded with an understanding look. "Trust takes a long time to build after it's been shattered. She might come around."

Vince took a chug and recalled her rejecting him. "I wouldn't count on it."

Angelo and Catherine exchange a glance. Angelo tapped the bar. "A new year is starting in an hour. The perfect time for new beginnings."

Vince had to drag himself up from brooding. He wasn't going to ruin their New Year's celebration by wallowing. "What do you two have planned for the year ahead?"

"Are you about to sound like Ma and ask if we'll be giving her any grandchildren soon?" Angelo drank his beer.

Catherine replied before Vince could respond. "Not yet. We're still in the newlywed period. Moving in together, adjusting to married life, and Angelo starting a new career outside of the Navy are big enough life challenges right now."

"Sounds like it," Vince replied. "I'm happy for you both." Vince pointed at their near empty glasses. "Are you ready for another round?"

The sound of sirens outside grabbed his attention. Seconds later the bright flashing lights of police cars streaked by the front windows of the bar. Soon after, two more cars passed.

Vince straightened, his senses naturally homed in to determine the threat level. With the number of them passing, something big must have been going on nearby.

"I'll be right back." Vince headed over to the front window, but with too many people squeezed into the bar, the view was blocked.

When he squeezed over to the front door, Angelo appeared beside him.

"It sounds like it's nearby. I'm going to see what's going on."

"I'm coming with you. Let me get Catherine."

"I'm right here." She stepped beside Angelo. "You two jumped to see what happened so quickly, like guard dogs respond when someone rings the doorbell."

"Sorry, babe. Can't turn it off, you know?" Angelo said.

Did that heightened level of awareness ever turn off?

"I understand," Catherine replied.

Vince squeezed out the front door and breathed in the cool night air, so refreshing after the heated congestion in the bar. Angelo was right behind him. Another police car drove by. Vince rushed in that direction, following the flashing lights around the corner. Half a dozen responders were parked in front of the hotel he'd just left—the hotel where he'd left Emma.

His heart stuttered. What the fuck was going on?

He ran to the hotel. He had to get to her and make sure she was safe.

CHAPTER TWENTY-ONE

EMMA

When she heard the order to evacuate, Emma thought it had to be a prank.

As she and Karine passed some first responders moving deeper into the hotel, the seriousness of the situation set in. Murmurs of voices grew louder as the crowd funneled out of the lobby that was as congested as salmon swimming upstream.

Concerned voices. Questions. Fear.

Once she finally exited the hotel, she gulped at the fresh air. So many flashing lights from police cars made her blink. A cool breeze hit her face.

"I'm glad you grabbed our coats." She took the coat Karine offered. A December night in Rhode Island wasn't exactly warm and cozy.

An officer directed them away from the hotel. As they followed the crowd, speculation grew louder—a bomb threat.

What?

The figure of a man rushing toward the hotel rather than

away from it made her mouth fall open. It was Vince.

She raised her hand and called out. "Vince! Vince!"

He didn't hear her. In the next second, he was swallowed by the shadows.

"Vince?" Karine repeated.

Emma's breathing grew more rapid. "He just ran toward the hotel." She pushed her way through the crowd, heading in that direction. "I need to get to him."

"You can't go back there." Karine grabbed her arm. "They won't let you in."

"But—but—" Her thoughts darted. "Why would he run into a hotel under evacuation?"

She answered her own question. He was an EOD tech. If it was a bomb threat, that was what he was trained to do.

"They probably won't let him in." Karine put her hand on Emma's shoulder. "We need to follow directions and get out of the way."

Emma nodded absently and wrapped her arms around her chest as Karine directed her away from the hotel. Her gaze traveled up the height of the hotel tower, which loomed over some smaller buildings nearby.

Please just let it be another hoax.

What if it was an actual bomb? Her pulse rocketed. He was in this situation because of her. He'd come here to reach out to her and how had she reacted—she'd asked him to *leave*. Her stomach churned.

"It's my fault he's here, Karine."

"No. Don't think that. You're not responsible for what's going on in there."

"He came here to talk to me, but I was too stubborn and scared. I could have at least said that we could talk about it tomorrow, and then he'd be headed back there, back to where he'd be safe." She raised a trembling hand to motion to the hotel. "Not there."

"Stop that, Emma." Karine used her let's-get-to-work voice. "If we're going to go down that road, then I'm just as much to blame because I told him where to find you. But we're *not* going to go down that path. Do you hear me? Because that's not going to help the situation."

Emma swallowed and nodded. "Okay, you're right. I don't know what to do. What should I do? How can I help him?"

"Exactly what you're doing. We need to get out of the way and let them do their jobs. This is what they are trained to handle."

Emma stood and rocked on the balls of her feet while her thoughts collided in her brain, ready to explode. Vince was right. He was nothing like Peter, nothing like her father. Vince dedicated his life to dealing with situations like this so he could help strangers, not expecting any thanks or accolades. He was incredibly brave and kind. Noble and honorable.

"He was right—and you're right," Emma said to Karine.

"About what?"

"I'm letting my past destroy my future."

"It's not too late to change that," Karine encouraged.

Right. What rose through the chaos in Emma's brain was that she had to ignore the fear of being hurt again and be brave like Vince. If he could rush headlong toward a hotel with a bomb threat, she could take one small step closer to him to see if they could make a relationship work.

She could do that.

Emma picked up the phone, but it went right to voice mail. Would he even hear his phone ring in this chaos?

She left a message.

"Vince, they told us to evacuate. I'm outside with Karine and saw you headed to the hotel. Please come meet me or let me know where I can find you." She glanced at their surroundings and noted the street they were heading down and some landmarks. Before she ended the call, she added, "Be careful."

VINCE

Vince ran toward the flashing of the police lights, heading for the main entrance. He had to get Emma.

People were rushing out of the lobby, and the police had already cordoned off the area with yellow tape.

He approached an officer. "I have to get inside. My girl—someone I care about is in there."

"I can't let you in," the young woman replied. "Everyone is being evacuated. You have to find her out here."

Fuuuckkk!

He walked away from the officer, trying to assess what he could from a distance. Where was Emma? He searched the crowd to look for a woman at her height with brown hair pulled up into a twist.

Damn it! If he hadn't tried to slow things down that night when he'd freaked out over the photos of O'Brien's family, they might have been having a different night together. If he'd manned up and asked her to go out on New Year's Eve, a symbolic night starting off a fresh new year together, she might not have been at this hotel tonight and in danger.

He'd let fear guide him and he had fucked it all up.

He glanced over to where he'd last seen his brother running toward an ambulance to offer his assistance as a paramedic. He spotted Angelo and jogged over to him.

"You okay?" Vince asked.

Angelo's nodded, but his expression was grim. He whispered, "Bomb threat."

Those two words made Vince's skin tingle as if a thousand microscopic bugs had buried into his flesh.

"Fuck." His stomach hollowed. The threat here in the States affecting someone he cared about hit him like he'd been run over by a tank. "I'm going over."

Angelo rubbed his beard. "I need to make sure Cate gets

home safe and then I'll be back."

Vince nodded and ran in search of a senior ranked member on the police force. Police dogs and their handlers entered the hotel, reminding him of his younger brother, Matty, a K-9 handler overseas with his SEAL team.

Near a police cruiser with lights flashing, Vince found a lieutenant who just ended a call.

Vince said, "I'm an EOD tech in the Marines. I heard it's a bomb threat and I can help."

The lieutenant nodded. "Thanks, but we have it covered."

Vince grimaced. Of course they did. This was their jurisdiction and they had their own SWAT teams and bomb units. These responders were likely well-trained and equipped to deal with the situation, so Vince couldn't interfere despite the raging drive to do so.

As Vince watched the scene unfolding before him, all his concerns about being in a relationship unraveled as easily as if it had been constructed by fragile threads. He'd been so convinced that he'd be the one whose life could be threatened during his time in the military, and that he could leave someone a widow, like O'Brien's wife. But shit could happen to anyone, anywhere. Robberies, active shooters, bomb threats...

Was he fooling himself hiding behind this fragile shell that shielded him from getting close to anyone?

O'Brien might have had it right. He'd lived his life to the fullest in the short time he had. He'd made others happy and had found happiness himself. It was time for Vince to man up and take a risk and *live* instead of watching life from a distance.

Another officer approached. "Sir, you need to leave the area."

Vince nodded in acknowledgment and backed away. No, he wasn't useless in this situation. He could do something. For someone.

Even if Emma didn't want him in her life, he could at least try to find her and get her to a safe place.

CHAPTER TWENTY-TWO

EMMA

Blocks down the road away from the hotel, Emma paced and touched her shamrock necklace.

"Can we pause for a second?" Emma asked Karine. "I want to text him."

"Sure." Karine pointed to a bench. "We've got to be close to half a mile from the hotel."

Far enough from a blast zone. But what about Vince?

Emma and Karine found a bench in front of a closed clothing store and waited. Late-night revelers passed them wearing New Year's crowns and talking loudly, oblivious to the situation at the hotel. Emma envied their ignorant bliss since anxiety gnawed on her every nerve.

She texted Vince with their location and added. *Please let me know where you are. Are you okay?*

Karine squeezed her shoulder. "There's nothing worse than wondering."

"It sucks," Emma agreed.

A small group of twenty-somethings nearby started the countdown. "10-9-8…"

Another group down the sidewalk joined in. Ah shit, she was caught in the cross-hairs of celebrations when she'd never felt less in the mood in her entire life.

"7-6-5-4-3-2-1."

"Happy New Year," Karine said.

Emma groaned. "Happy New Year," she mumbled. If there was a prize for the most lackadaisical declaration, she'd have won it. "Sorry, I don't feel like celebrating."

"I know. Just trying to distract you."

People kissed and embraced. More "Happy New Year" sentiments followed. Emma stared at a crack in the sidewalk, hoping the moment would soon pass and people would move on.

It took several more ice ages before that happened.

A man strode with purpose through a group of meandering teens. Her heart revved and kickstarted like she was in a Motley Crue video. She touched her necklace and stood. Was this a dream?

"Oh my God, he's okay."

Karine rose. "Where is he?"

Emma pointed. "Right there." She ran over to Vince.

As she approached, their eyes locked, and she froze. She took in a sharp breath and it lodged somewhere in her throat.

He took a step towards her. "Emma, you're okay."

"Of course." She smiled. "You're the one who went running into danger."

"I had to make sure you were okay."

Her hands trembled as she covered her heart. "Vince…"

"I got your message and rushed here as fast as I could."

She closed the remaining feet between them and threw her arms around his neck. "I was such an idiot. A coward. Forget everything I said earlier."

He pressed one hand to her back and then cradled her

against his chest. "I'm the idiot who got scared earlier and screwed this all up."

"Yeah, you're both a couple of idiots," Karine quipped. "But that was last year. It's a new year, a new start for everyone."

Emma pulled back, her eyes brimming with tears of relief. "You're right, Karine."

Karine replied with a sage nod. "Of course I'm right." She grinned and then waved, "Now get out of here and start the new year off right together."

Emma furrowed her brows. "What about everything that's going on at the hotel?"

"I'll deal with it if they deem it safe and let us back in. Besides, I brought you both into this situation by asking you to help tonight. So lessen my guilt by going and having some fun together."

"I'd suggest you head home too," Vince added. "It's a big hotel and it will take a while for them to clear it."

"Right. Good idea," Karine replied. "Good night."

Emma hugged her. "Thank you. And Happy New Year." She put more into it this time rather than the pathetic sentiment she'd uttered earlier.

After Karine walked away, Emma turned to Vince. "What do you say?"

VINCE

Vince stared into Emma's hopeful eyes and so many emotions bounced through his chest. Most of all gratitude and relief. She was safe.

"There's nothing else I'd rather do than go anywhere with you."

She sighed. "I was so scared I might never see you again."

He brushed a strand of hair off her cheek and behind her ear. "Same here."

Tears pooled in the corners of her eyes. "I know you're not my ex or my father. You're you, Vince. The bravest and most considerate man I know. I regret letting my issues blind me until now."

"Everyone has issues." Vince swallowed. "Demons. We know each other's now and I have nothing more to hide. Do you think we can deal with them together?"

She nodded and grinned through glistening eyes. "Yes."

A tear rolled down her cheek, and he wiped it away. "You okay?"

"Yes." She dabbed her eyes with the back of her hand. "Just give me a minute."

"Of course." He glanced over his shoulder in the direction of the hotel. No sign of Angelo. "I better tell my brother what's going on."

Emma clutched him as if reluctant to let him go, but then released him. He kissed her forehead and then texted Angelo.

Found Emma outside. We're both safe.

After thirty seconds, Angelo responded, *The things you'll do to get the girl...*

Ha. You okay?

Yeah, I'm with Cate. Where are you?

Vince texted their location. A few minutes later, Angelo and Catherine turned from around a corner.

"There's my brother and sister-in-law," he pointed out to Emma.

Once he introduced them, they exchanged quick greetings.

"What a night to meet," Catherine noted.

"Exactly." Emma nodded.

"I got some intel." Angelo glanced at Emma and explained, "I'm a first responder here." Then he turned to Vince. "A man had called in the bomb threat. He demanded money or said he'd blow up the hotel. It wasn't a hoax this time. They found one in the boiler room and neutralized it. They're still searching to make sure there aren't any others."

"Shit." Vince covered his mouth and lowered his arm to his side. "I should go back."

"Vince," Angelo said in his common sense, big brother voice.

Right. Vince had to accept that some things were out of his control.

Besides, Emma might need him. He sure as hell needed her.

"Yeah, you're right. I'll just get in the way."

Angelo nodded. "I'm going to stand by a bit longer, just in case."

Right, if shit went down, they might need a paramedic.

"It's been a long night," Angelo added. "Do you both want to crash at our place?"

"We have a sofa bed and an inflatable mattress—whichever you'd find more comfortable," Catherine offered.

"Thanks for the hospitality, but I think I need the comfort of my own bed," Emma replied.

"I'm going to head back to Newport as well. Happy New Year." Vince hugged Angelo and Catherine. "Thanks for coming down tonight."

"Happy New Year," Angelo replied.

Emma and Catherine repeated it as well.

After they walked in opposite directions, Vince slung his arm around Emma.

She leaned into him, resting her head on his side. "Are you coming with me back to my place?"

"If you want me there."

"I do."

He exhaled. "Good. All I care about is that we're together, and that you're giving me a second chance."

She turned and smiled up at him. "It's a new year. And there's nobody I'd rather start it with than you, Vince."

He turned and stared into her eyes—so beautiful and filled

with warmth and appreciation. He'd never do anything to break her trust, knowing how hard it had been to be earned.

He caressed her cheek. "In that case, I think we should start it out properly."

"Oh, and how's that?"

"3-2-1. Happy New Year." He bent down and met her lips in a kiss to start their new year together, hoping it was the first of many.

EPILOGUE

VINCE

Christmas Eve
Emma put down her final Scrabble letter, ending the game with cheers in Vince's parents' living room.

"Let me add up the final scores." Angelo grabbed a pen and tallied up the points. "Looks like it's Vince with a narrow lead."

More loudness ensued. What a difference from last Christmas when he'd been stuck on that damn puzzle while consumed by thoughts of Emma. Now she was here with him, happy to take part in limoncello and game time with his family. Since they'd be back again tomorrow, it was enough family time. He had plans and it involved spending time alone with her.

"We're gonna get going," he said.

"So early?" His mother protested. "We're having such a good time."

"Which will continue tomorrow," his father added.

Neither of his parents played the four-person game, saying

they'd watch, but Vince wouldn't have thought it with all their "helpful" suggestions during the game. That was just like them, and it made him smile. Too bad Matty couldn't make it back this Christmas. Maybe next year.

"We should head out too," Angelo added.

His mother's mouth opened, as if ready to protest.

"Let them go, Marissa. Everyone will be back tomorrow."

"Everything was delicious," Emma added, capturing his mother's attention.

"Thank you." His mother beamed. "Make sure you're here by three tomorrow."

"We will be." Emma hugged his mother, and then Vince followed suit.

An hour later, Vince carried hot chocolates with candy canes into Emma's living room. She brought over a small bag of chocolate chip cookies that Karine had dropped off earlier. The sweet scents and those of the pine tree infused her place with the scents of Christmas.

They had picked out a giant tree together, which didn't fit into her apartment without him sawing off four inches from the trunk. A few nights ago, they had decorated it together. He never thought a domestic holiday tradition could bring him such happiness.

Once they settled onto the couch, Emma picked up the remote and turned on the TV. "*A Christmas Story?*"

"Of course." Vince remembered last Christmas Eve when he had ended up here after Emma had been spooked by the break-in. She had fallen asleep in his arms while they watched the movie. This year he wanted to create a new memory for them and wipe away any of the negative ones that might linger in her mind.

"I'm so glad you were able to come home again this Christmas." She turned and glanced at him. "Especially since we don't know if you can make it home next year."

"I'll do my best."

They'd spent the past year trying to see each other as often as possible, which generally worked out to two weekends a month. He'd fly up to Newport or she'd come down to visit him at Camp Lejeune in North Carolina. But he had orders to ship to Okinawa, Japan, all the way on the other side of the world from Emma. Too far from her.

They sipped the hot cocoa and ate the cookies while they watched the movie. He adjusted his position several times.

After several minutes, Emma glanced at him with furrowed brows. "What's going on, Vince? You can't seem to sit still."

Nerves, that's what. What he was about to do was huge, something he'd never considered with anyone before.

And it could blow up in his face.

He took the remote and turned off the TV. He then grabbed a different remote to play Christmas music. Frank Sinatra's "I'll Be Home for Christmas" played, one that always choked him up when he had been away during the holidays. But this year, he was home—because he was with Emma.

"Must be this thing in my pocket." He stood and made a show of pulling the small box out before he lowered himself to one knee.

Emma covered her mouth with both hands and gasped.

He took one of her hands. "Emma, I'm so grateful to have you in my life and will never take for granted how you've been there for me. I know being with a jarhead isn't easy."

She laughed. "True."

"I've fallen so deeply in love with you and want to be with you, however you'll have me. I'd love for you to come to Okinawa with me but understand if you don't want to. If I need to leave the Marines when my tour is up, you've got it. You're my future now. Whatever makes you happy, sign me up because that is what you've made me."

"Oh, Vince." She placed a hand on her heart.

He sucked in a breath before continuing. "Emma Bradford, will you marry me?"

He opened the box with the marquise diamond set in white gold and offered it to her.

Her eyes glistened. "Yes!"

Vince's eyes widened. An elated sense of lightness filled his chest. Did he hear correctly or just imagine it from rehearsing this so many times before tonight? "Yes?"

"Of course, yes." One side of her mouth turned up into a grin. "I love you, Vince. You made it kind of hard not to."

His hands were shaking as he slid the ring on her finger. He couldn't believe she said yes. After he rose, he whooped and wrapped her in his arms before he twirled her. Once he set her on her feet, he cupped her cheeks, searched her bright eyes, and kissed her. It was slow and unhurried, but soon left them both breathless.

After she pulled back, she said, "And yes, I want to go to Japan with you."

His eyes widened. "You do?"

She cocked her head and gazed at him. "I'd much rather explore a new country with you than stay here missing you."

"Oh, Emma." He kissed her again. "Thank you."

She grinned. "One request if it's possible. Can we live off base?"

He didn't know all the particulars with family housing but knew of a couple who lived in a great little apartment in a residential area the last time he'd been there. "I'll look into our options."

"Perfect." She nodded. "And after this tour ends, we'll figure it out together."

He nodded. "Right. From now on, we decide on our future together."

For someone who enjoyed spending so much time alone, *together* never sounded so blissful.

"How do you think your mother will take the news today?" Emma tilted her head with a smile.

"She's going to be insanely happy, fretting all over you. The pressure for grandchildren will be *on*."

Emma laughed. "Karine will flip out with excitement as well."

Vince cocked his head. "Hmm, should we enlist her for some cupcakes at our wedding?"

"Right. Her confectionery creations are critical." Emma arched a brow and her eyes glimmered.

He chuckled at the alliteration, a nod to the first time they'd met over fallen cupcakes at Angelo and Catherine's wedding. "I have an idea if you're up for it."

"Another good idea, I hope."

"I'm thinking we should go away for the new year—just the two of us."

After what had happened last New Year's Eve, a quiet escape sounded perfect. They'd arrested the man responsible. A disgruntled worker who had been fired from the hotel had called in bomb threats to gauge the response before following through with an actual one and a demand for cash.

"What do you have in mind?"

"We could head up to the White Mountains. Maybe some cross-country skiing. A little cabin in the woods. Just you and me."

Emma nodded and then gave him a luminous smile. "That sounds like the perfect start to a new year together with my fiancé."

"Fiancé," he repeated. "I like the sound of that." He leaned down and kissed her again. "It's time we make some new memories and traditions. Together."

"Then I have the perfect date for our wedding." She peered at him with a bright gleam in her eyes.

He knew what she was thinking as they now spoke in that

secret communication he'd seen with other couples. "New Year's Eve?"

"If we can make it happen, let's do it." She then took his hand and led him to the bedroom. "How about some alone time right now?"

MATTY

Nine Months Later...

Matty caught the damn garter. Shit.

He hadn't meant to do so and had even stood off to the side in the back row. He gaped at Vince who watched with a sly grin. Had it been intentional for him to throw it at Matty? Probably. When it had come at him, he had instinctively reached out to catch it.

Cheers followed, with the loudest coming from Angelo. He strode over with Vince and patted him on the back. "Hey brother," he used the tone that Matty used when quoting Buster from *Arrested Development*. "Looks like you're next!"

"Ha, funny. It's just some silly wedding tradition."

"No, no, no." Angelo waved his hand. "I've seen it happen. The guy who catches the garter indeed ends up being the next one to get married. Right, Vince?"

Vince nodded with a straight face. "True."

Matty's gut hollowed. "It's just a superstition," he scoffed. "Just because my brothers have gotten soft, doesn't mean I'm going to follow their lead."

"Why not? You followed us both into the military," Vince noted.

"That's different. And then I went my own way." Being a K-9 handler was nothing like what either of his brothers did in the service.

"Never say never." Angelo raised his index finger. "When you meet the right woman, strange things can happen, changing what you thought you wanted."

Matty forced a grin. "We'll see." He grabbed his beer from the nearby table. He was going to need ten more if there was anything to that superstition.

Nah, it was just his brothers messing with him. He'd already heard the "You're next" line countless times tonight. Now that he'd caught the garter, he was going to get hell about his fate.

Matty glanced at his sixteen-year-old cousin who had caught the bouquet. She covered part of it with her hand, apparently horrified that a relative had caught it.

Oh well, time to slap on a smile and put on a show. He could do that. It was less intense than heading into hostile territory to search for explosives.

Right?

He strode over to Ayla. Her face turned red showing her mortification. He'd make a joke about it to make her feel more comfortable.

The DJ stopped him. "Oh no, no, no. You can't just walk over to her. You need to put a little effort into it. A little show." He switched to the Hot Chocolate song, *You Sexy Thing*.

Angelo and Vince roared with laughter along with their cousins, Jack and Antonio, who were both Marines from Boston. Great.

Matty snapped his fingers and wiggled his hips, putting on the performance that everyone wanted to see—everyone except for Ayla that was. She turned away, mouthing with mock horror to her sisters. Matty shifted toward his brothers and cousins, who were the ones who really wanted the show. He jumped and turned 180-degrees and then twerked for them. They hollered and cheered.

Matty finished shaking his ass and then strode back to Ayla. "Don't worry, the worst is over."

"On her ankle," the DJ directed. "She's family."

Matty slid the garter on her.

Ayla skittered off the second the deed was done, rushing back to her sisters. "That was so embarrassing!"

Matty laughed. He turned to face the still boisterous crew and bent forward with an dramatic bow.

"Nice moves, DeMarchis," Jack said.

"I try."

"You'll need them for your wedding night," Antonio added.

Matty walked away with an exaggerated prowl to complete his performance. With a casual glance over his shoulder, he added, "This tiger is not ready to be tamed."

AUTHOR'S NOTE:

Find out what happens next when Matty runs into Jenna, his best friend's little sister, when he's back in Newport. When Matty and Jenna pretend to be a couple to convince her ex that she's moved on, a fake relationship with someone off limits is more difficult than he anticipated. Read more in Matty's story in the Anchor Me series!

BE A VIP READER!

Join us in the Lisa Carlisle Readers Facebook group!

Visit lisacarlislebooks.com to subscribe to my reader newsletter and see the latest releases. New readers receive a welcome gift, exclusive bonus

ACKNOWLEDGMENTS

I'm always grateful for every person I'm in contact with as I work on a new book. It takes many rounds of revision to get the shape the story in my head into one that works on the page. I had many questions answered by a professor at the Naval War College, a police lieutenant in New England, and a Marine who served more recently than me. I appreciate all their feedback to add realistic details and scenarios to the story. Note this story and the characters are entirely fictional.

As always, tremendous thanks to my critique group, editor, beta readers, proofreader, ARC readers, and you, the reader! Thank you for spending time with me with characters I love.

Lisa

ABOUT THE AUTHOR

USA Today bestselling author Lisa Carlisle loves to write stories about wounded or misunderstood heroes finding their happily ever after. They often face the temptation of fated and forbidden love--so difficult to resist!

Her romances have been named Top Picks at Night Owl Reviews and the Romance Reviews.

She draws on her travels and experiences in her stories, which include deploying to Okinawa, Japan, while in the Marines, backpacking alone through Europe, and living in Paris before returning to the U.S. She owned a bookstore for a few years as she loves to read. She's now married to a fantastic man, and they have two kids, two cats, and too many fish.

Visit her website for more on books, trailers, playlists, and more:
Lisacarlislebooks.com

Sign up for her newsletter to hear about new releases, specials, and freebies:
http://www.lisacarlislebooks.com/subscribe/

Lisa loves to connect with readers. You can find her on:

Facebook
Twitter

Pinterest
Instagram
Goodreads

BOOK LIST

Anchor Me

Navy SEALs, Marines, and hometown heroes. Each one encounters his most complicated mission yet, when he will find a woman from his past—who changes his future.

- *Antonio (a novella available for free to subscribers!)*
- *Angelo*
- *Vince*
- *Matty*
- *Jack*

Underground Encounters

Steamy paranormal romances set in an underground goth club that attracts vampires, witches, shifters, and gargoyles.

- *Book 1: SMOLDER (a vampire / firefighter romance)*
- *Book 2: FIRE (a witch / firefighter romance)*
- *Book 3: IGNITE (a feline shifter / rock star romance)*
- *Book 4: BURN (a vampire / shapeshifter rock romance)*
- *Book 5: HEAT (a gargoyle shifter romance)*
- *Book 6: BLAZE (a gargoyle shifter rockstar romance)*
- *Book 7: COMBUST (vampire / witch romances)*
- *Book 8: INFLAME (a gargoyle shifter / witch romance)*
- *Book 9: TORCH (a gargoyle shifter / werewolf romance*
- *Book 10: SCORCH (an incubus vs succubus demon romance)*

Chateau Seductions

An art colony on a remote New England island lures creative types—

and supernatural characters. Steamy paranormal romances.

- *Darkness Rising*
- *Dark Velvet*
- *Dark Muse*
- *Dark Stranger*
- *Dark Pursuit*

Highland Gargoyle

Gargoyle shifters, wolf shifters, and tree witches have divided the Isle of Stone after a great battle 25 years ago. One risk changes it all…

- *Knights of Stone: Mason*
- *Knights of Stone: Lachlan*
- *Knights of Stone: Bryce*
- *Seth: a wolf shifter romance in the series*
- *Knights of Stone: Calum*
- *Stone Cursed*
- *Knights of Stone: Gavin*

Stone Sentries

Meet your perfect match the night of the super moon — or your perfect match for the night. A cop teams up with a gargoyle shifter when demons attack Boston.

- *Tempted by the Gargoyle*
- *Enticed by the Gargoyle*
- *Captivated by the Gargoyle*

Night Eagle Operations

A paranormal romantic suspense novel

- *When Darkness Whispers*

Berkano Vampires

A shared author world with dystopian paranormal romances.

- *Immortal Resistance*

Blood Courtesans

A shared author world with the vampire blood courtesans.

- *Pursued: Mia*

Visit LisaCarlisleBooks.com to learn more!

Printed in Great Britain
by Amazon